Mad

Marshal Bronco Madigan found Cadey after a long hunt and earned two more bullet scars for his collection. But Cadey got religion and opened up a ten-year-old can of worms that brought Chief Marshal Miles Parminter storming out of his Washington office, primed for trouble.

But, in the field, he had to rely on Madigan's talents with gun and fists to track down the most terrifying outlaw the West had ever seen – or was likely to see. There were hostile lawmen, crooked lawmen and killer lawmen – and there was Madigan's kind of lawman.

The kind who didn't quit until the job was done – or he was dead.

Madigan's Star

HANK J. KIRBY

A Black Horse Western

ROBERT HALE · LONDON

ISBN 0 7090 7024 1

Robert Hale Limited
Clerkenwell House
Clerkenwell Green
London EC1R 0HT

Typeset by
Derek Doyle & Associates, Liverpool.
Printed and bound in Great Britain by
Antony Rowe Limited, Wiltshire.

1
Confession

The window burst outwards, glass spraying amongst long slivers of humming wood, the frame ripping loose some of the clapboards of the wall.

A man hurtled through the ragged gap, somersaulting in mid-air like an acrobat, landing on his feet but stumbling. He put down one hand and with a flick of strong, flexible fingers pushed himself upright, the forward momentum carrying him almost to the stack of crates and old barrels. He grunted as he stretched muscles and flung himself at the only shelter available, hit the dirt hard and rolled in behind the nearest barrel.

As he did so two bullets ripped into the strong, curved wood, splinters flying, the keg moving a few inches. The man wiped sweat from his eyes and bared his teeth briefly, panting. His hands fumbled the sixgun out of his waistband and he thumbed home fresh cartridges taken from his torn shirt-pocket. There were only four, but one would be

5

enough if only he could draw bead on that son of a bitch who was trying to kill him!

There he was now, crouching at the hole in the wall, rifle smoking as his hard eyes sought his quarry amongst the crates and empty barrels; there was nowhere else to hide.

'You run, Cadey, and I'll swat you like a fly!' called Bronco Madigan, US marshal. For effect he clashed the lever of the rifle, ejecting the fired casing as a new load slid home. 'Step out with your hands up and I'll take you in.'

'What for? Just to be hung?'

'You'll be alive for a few weeks yet. There'll be the ride back, your trial, sentencing. Man, life's too good to end it here and now with a bullet.'

'Better than a goddamn rope! You go to hell, Madigan.'

'Reckon I'll see you there but you'll be first, if that's the way you want it.'

'I – don't have a choice, damn you!'

'I just gave you one. You didn't want it. Now, die!'

Cadey crouched low, shaking as he wiped his gun-hand down his trousers, then took the weapon in a firmer grip. *If only he could take Madigan with him! Well – he aimed to make a damned good try at doing just that . . .*

Any other thoughts he had were suddenly cut short.

Something glowing arced from the busted window and he watched in almost dreamy fascination as a lighted lantern sailed towards his hiding place, struck the barrel next to the one he was using as

6

cover and burst. A sheet of flame engulfed the old liquor kegs in a second and Cadey yelled as the sleeve of his shirt caught fire. He slapped at it and must have exposed a part of his body briefly because the lawman's rifle cracked and Cadey spun to the ground as lead ripped across the point of his left shoulder.

He was agile, though, and there was no real pain yet, only the sensation of a hammer-blow and a kind of stinging. He rolled, kicking at one of the blazing barrels, sending it clattering back towards the trading post where Madigan sheltered. Scrabbling on all fours, he lurched away, trying to keep the blazing heap of trash between him and the marshal.

Madigan cursed: his plan had rebounded. The damn stack of crates and barrels had caught fire all right, and he had flushed Cadey, but now he couldn't see the man because of the leaping flames and smoke and heat distortion.

He dived through the shattered window, shoulder-rolling, and ended up facing the flames, but off to one side. He glimpsed Cadey, up and running, left arm dangling; down on one knee, Madigan got the rifle to his shoulder and triggered. Dust and gravel erupted in a long line ahead and to the right of the running fugitive. Madigan rammed home another cartridge, the foresight following Cadey as the man desperately weaved from side to side as he stretched out for the line of trees and the stream beyond.

Lifting above those trees were the white walls and single tower of the San Mateo mission.

And suddenly Madigan knew that Cadey was going

7

to try and make it to the mission, ask for sanctuary from the reverend fathers – and he would get it. And Madigan wouldn't be able to do anything about it. Hell, he was already in Mexico illegally. . . .

He slowed, breath banging in his throat, chest heaving, forcing himself to drag down air more steadily. He had been chasing Cadey for days and this last time had been going on for more than half an hour. He held out his right hand. It wasn't rock steady like it once would have been.

Getting old, he thought bitterly.

But he watched with narrowed eyes as Cadey's long legs ate the distance to the tree-line. He'd be there in ten seconds more. Madigan sucked down a good, deep breath, held it, even as the rifle came up and the brass-bound butt settled snugly into his shoulder. He swung the barrel ahead of Cadey, up to the tree-line, back to the running man, judged he needed to lead by about two feet. He settled the blade foresight level with the tips of the rear buckhorn, already taking up the first slack in the trigger. *By God, it was going to be close!*

Cadey was almost there, and his body took on a stiff, jarring posture as he made the final effort to reach the shelter of the trees.

Madigan fired.

The smoke obscured his target briefly and when he stepped to one side impatiently he couldn't see Cadey. He swore aloud, unable to believe he had missed at that range.

No! There was the son of a bitch! On the ground, stretched out, still skidding through the short,

8

parched grass. One leg half-doubled under him as he used it to propel his body under the brush-line just this side of the first trees. Madigan's rifle came up and he fired the last remaining three shots in the magazine, seeing the leaves and twigs flying.

Cadey's body jumped even as the man rolled beneath the bush. Madigan thumbed home four shells from his belt through the rifle's loading-gate, watching all the time. But there must have been a small hollow, for Cadey had dropped out of sight.

He levered the rifle and started forward at a half-trot, approaching side-on so as to make a smaller target, crouching a little. No movement there. No sign of the fugitive. The birds were beginning to call again now the gunfire had died away.

But no birds flitted about the brush where Cadey had disappeared. Something was there they didn't trust.

Madigan didn't trust it, either. He knew Cadey of old. The man was tough as they come; he might be hit, more than once, too, but he had chosen to go down fighting and that's the way he would make it happen. The man's main aim now would be to take Madigan to hell with him.

But Madigan had no intention of going there, just yet.

He crouched down even more, approached with careful, long strides, working around to the right so he could get a look beneath the bush. It was deeply shadowed and he couldn't make out any movement. But it was almost up against the base of a tree and it was possible that Cadey just might have managed to get behind that thick trunk. From his original approach, Madigan wouldn't have been able to see the movement.

But he saw movement now!

Just a slight flicking at the edge of his vision and he realized he was looking at the wrong tree. Cadey had somehow managed to get to the tree *next* to what would have been the logical one for him to use.

But then Cadey always had been cunning-smart.

The thought flashed through Madigan's mind even as he swung the rifle up and across to the new tree, but Cadey stepped out, left hand pressed into his bloody side, more blood streaking his face from a head wound, his Colt already blazing.

Madigan jerked and fell, triggering, as something seared across his neck and almost tore his head from his shoulders. He saw his first shot kick a handful of bark from the tree trunk above Cadey's head and then, as the scene faded behind a red mist, he jammed the rifle's butt against his hip and worked lever and trigger until the hammer clicked again and again on an empty breach.

By that time he was down on his knees, blinking, trying to clear his vision – and seeing Cadey leaning against the tree, bloody and pale, but baring his teeth in triumph as he raised his Colt in both hands, cocked the hammer, and . . .

The last thing Madigan saw was the ragged sword of flame leaping from the Colt's muzzle.

Limbo. . . .

There was a period in limbo, a place he had been

before – and didn't like. It was too full of bad dreams and sweaty chases through cloying swamps where the trees themselves seemed to snatch at him and try to hold him for whatever was in pursuit.

He saw too many dead men.

Men he had killed. . . .

But limbo ended eventually and he found himself in a small bare room lying on a hard narrow bunk. There was a terracotta jug of water on a crude wooden stool within reach and he drank deeply, immediately grabbed at his throat because it hurt so much to swallow. Then he felt the bandages around his neck and shortly after that he remembered his pursuit of Cadey.

He wondered if the man had got away.

Shortly afterwards, a man in a long brown robe came into his room – more like a cell, really – smiled, made the sign of the cross over him and immediately knelt and prayed at bedside. Then he looked up and said in fluent, though accented American,

'I am thanking God for sparing your life, *sénor* – I fear the other man will not survive.'

'Cadey?' Madigan was startled to hear his voice. Well, what passed for his voice now. It was scratchy, hoarse, no more than a whisper no matter how much he tried to make it louder.

The mission brother placed a hand gently on his shoulder and pushed him back as he tried to raise himself.

'You must relax, my son. Your voice will return soon. You grow stronger each day but your leg may trouble you.'

11

'How – long – here?' grated Madigan, gesturing to the cell, knowing he was in the mission.

'Three days. The other man must be very strong to hold on. He is almost blind from the head wound, but it is the body wounds that are slowly killing him.'

'Must – see him!'

The brother shook his head. 'Not yet. I know you are an American lawman – and the other man must be an outlaw, but to us at San Mateo he is a man first, and we must care for him. He has asked for sanctuary and we have granted it, but I fear he will soon find his sanctuary with God.'

'Not that one! More likely with Satan.'

The brother smiled, said he would send food later and in the meantime Madigan should rest.

He did for a time. About an hour, then food was brought to him, mostly a thick gruel-like liquid in a wooden bowl and bread without crust. He appreciated that after the first swallow.

He felt better after eating and within twenty minutes he was standing and walking slowly around the cell, using the walls for support. He saw through the one glassless window that it was early evening.

A bell began to toll and soon hymns and prayers echoed through the cold white walls of the mission. The brothers would soon be in their own cells, praying before going to sleep. *He could wait that long.* . . .

It took Madigan only fifteen minutes to find Cadey's cell.

The wounded lawman was dressed in a brown robe

he had found hanging on a nail behind the door of his room, gathered around his waist with a length of rope. There was no collar and the edges of the white throat-bandage showed above the coarse-weave cloth. He dragged his left leg a little, the wound in his thigh causing him a deal of pain.

No doors were locked and he opened them carefully, looking in. Most of the rooms had a candle-stub burning before a small altar or statuary set up by the occupants as their own private place of worship. The seventh room had a candle burning, too, but there was no altar or statues of Christ.

Only Cadey, groaning on his narrow bed, sweating, murmuring incoherently. Madigan went in swiftly, head spinning with the sudden movement and closed the door gently behind him. Cadey heard the movement and the rustle of the brown robe as Madigan limped towards the bed.

The damp hair and moist face gleamed dully in the flickering, dim light of the candle-stub and the dark, sunken eyes widened. A hand groped feebly towards Madigan.

'Father!'

The lawman frowned as Cadey's fingers tore at the robe, tugging. Madigan was quite weak himself and had to shuffle to keep his balance, but sat on the edge of the narrow bed, Cadey's burning gaze on his face constantly.

'Can't see – properly – I – I'm dyin', Father! I – know it . . .'

Madigan started to speak but his throat hurt and he swallowed, put a hand to the bandages showing

13

above the neck of the robe. He wondered if it looked like a priest's collar to Cadey. Just a band of white above the neckline . . . *which would explain why he had called him 'Father'.*

'Rest easy,' grated Madigan experimentally, watching Cadey's face closely.

He was surprised to see the outlaw's features slacken and relax, a lot of tension going out of his eyes.

'Mighty glad – I can talk with you, Father! I – I got a lot on my conscience – terrible things I want to – to confess. Will you hear my confession, Father? Please. . .?'

Madigan was uncomfortable, and angry because he didn't know why. But this was too good an opportunity to pass up and he lifted one hand and made a clumsy sign of the cross over the dying Cadey.

'Confess your sins, my son, and you will be forgiven . . .'

He hoped that sounded right.

Cadey lay back and almost smiled, closing his eyes and for a wild moment Madigan thought the man had already died, but then the gasping voice spoke.

'I've killed and raped and stole, Father, and I've committed every sin in the book – but I – I ain't as bad – *evil* – as another feller named Griffin—'

'Mathias Griffin?' Madigan grated before he could stop himself.

But Cadey merely nodded, not wondering how a supposed mission father would know the name of the terrible outlaw. But Madigan knew the name. He also knew Griffin had died ten years ago, so why was

Cadey talking about him now? Madigan was more interested in Cadey's recent doings, with the gang of outlaws who had held up the Lincolnville mail train and killed two guards and a passenger.

'I shared a cell with him,' Cadey said. Madigan reached out, tight-lipped, and patted the man's arm.

'That must have been a long time ago, my son. Try to stick with your most recent sins. Have you broken the law lately?'

Cadey snorted, coughed, gasped, thrashed and his eyes flew wide and Madigan thought he was gone. But he settled down again, clawed tightly at Madigan's robe.

'God's law, man's law – I – I've broke 'em all! But – I – I can't let – Griff – loose . . . not – someone like – him. Not – right. . . .'

Dammit! The man's raving! He's gonna die before he tells me anything useful. . . .

'Tell me about the train robbery – my son.' He threw that last in as an afterthought. But it did no good.

Cadey clawed the robe so hard he was trying to pull himself erect. His words became slurred.

'Father! Father! I – I ain't got much – time. There's a – US marshal – name of Par – Parminter. Tell him – Griffin's – still alive – an' – the – monster's – comin' – out . . .'

The voice faded and Cadey slumped on the bunk and Madigan knew it was the last anyone in this world would hear from the man.

He stood and looked down at the dead outlaw, lifted a hand, almost as if he was going to make a sign of the cross above him but he rested the hand against the wall for support and gave Cadey his final blessing.

    '*Rot in hell, Cadey!*'

2
Griffin

The hip wound didn't heal as fast as the rest of Madigan's injuries although the bad bullet-burn in his neck ran a close second as far as healing-time was concerned.

He stayed at the mission and Brother Ignatius, the one who had been assigned to looking after him, agreed to send a telegram to Chief Marshal Miles Parminter in Washington. Madigan wrote the message partly in code, partly in plain language. It read like a brief report on his situation, adding that Cadey was dead and including the information about Griffin.

Madigan had no idea why Cadey had figured it was important for Parminter to know, but some hunch told him the sooner he passed on the news the better. Anyway, Parminter, being in Washington with the entire Marshals' Service at his disposal, was in a far better position to investigate – if he felt it needed investigating.

17

Madigan was surprised and not a little angry to find that he wasn't recovering as quickly as he would have liked. He was just past the forty mark: that seemingly magical number in the human race's supposed three score years and ten, and he was finding more creaks and stiffness in his muscles every day lately. Especially after a hard ride or a fight. Once he would have met each day feeling like he could walk through a brick wall while making a cigarette and have it lighted by the time the bricks had stopped falling. Now when he awoke of a morning he wondered if he would have enough energy to kick in the sides of a wet paper bag.

Getting old, he told himself.

But it acted as a spur, made him push himself more than he would normally and he had many an argument with Brother Ignatius about it. Usually the brother won – simply by locking him in by means of a bar across the outside of the cell door.

So Madigan settled into a routine devised by the good brother and found that the man's herbs and mission-made unguents seemed to work. His voice was returning more strongly but he still had a deep kind of grate there that hadn't been present before Cadey's bullet had wounded him. He knew how lucky he was: if the bullet had moved a bare half-inch to the left it would have torn his head off. As it was, he would have yet another scar to carry to his grave.

The thigh wound handicapped him because the bullet had damaged the muscle and he was forced to walk using, first a crutch for a week, and then a walking-stick, both implements hand-carved by other members of the mission. There were about twenty of them altogether as far as he could tell. They smiled at him, blessed him with handsigns, prayed for him, but rarely spoke – except for Brother Ignatius. When he asked about it, Ignatius merely smiled and said,

'They keep their words for God. Besides, I am the only one who speaks your language fluently.'

It was two and a half weeks before Brother Ignatius gave in to Madigan's incessant nagging and agreed he could leave the mission. The marshal gave what money he had to the mission and when Ignatius tried to give him some back, he shook his head.

'I can ride all right, Brother – and I can wire for more funds once I get to El Paso. Mebbe I'll send you some more after I get back to Washington. I'm mighty beholden to you and the others here at San Mateo.'

'It is only God's work we do, my son, there is no need for thanks. But, instead of money, perhaps you could send us wood-carving tools? Or a small crucible for our foundry?'

Madigan agreed. 'Whatever you want, Brother.' He shook hands and, still using the walking-stick mainly for the other's benefit, made his way to where they had his horse waiting, the packs bulging with food and a few small gifts.

He had trouble mounting but Ignatius helped him, smiling gently. 'If you should wish to return – for a little more recuperation – do so before you reach the sierras, otherwise you will not reach here before dark.'

Fighting to hold back a grimace as he worked the

foot of his wounded left leg into the stirrup, Madigan forced a smile and touched two fingers to the brim of his battered, trail-stained hat.

'*Adios*, Brother. You ever in El Paso, or need help, go to the US marshal's office there. They'll know where to find me.'

Brother Ignatius made the sign of the cross.

'Ride far, ride well, Señor Madigan. May God and your star watch over you.'

Madigan frowned. 'God I know about. But the only star I follow is this one.' He touched the brass star within the circle tugging at his shirt-pocket.

'Of course it isn't. Every man has a star to lead him through life to his final reward.'

'Now don't go deep on me, Brother!' said the lawman. He wheeled his mount and began to ride away, lifting the horse to a canter.

He regretted it almost immediately because of the jarring through his leg, but he gritted his teeth and kept up the pace until he reached the stream, when he had an excuse for slowing down.

Standing at the mission gate, Brother Ignatius smiled slowly and turned back to resume his normal life. He couldn't help but feel it would be just a little more boring now that Bronco Madigan was gone.

The *americano* was a violent man, hard of mind and body, but there was an innate decency in him, even though he tried his best to hide it.

Perhaps the only star he followed *was* the one he had pinned to his shirt. Certainly it seemed to be the only life he knew – or wanted.

*

Bronco Madigan was sure glad to reach El Paso.

It wasn't that it had been such a long ride from the San Mateo mission, but it had *seemed* endless and his left leg felt as if it was falling off. Fact was, several times he wished to hell it *would* fall off and then maybe he would get some relief from the constant nagging pain.

But when he made camp he heated extra water as Brother Ignatius had advised him to do, soaked a cloth in the steaming liquid, and wrapped a handful of mixed herbs – supplied by the brothers – in the wet folds. Several applications of this herbal heat, followed by cold-water packs usually eased the pain and stiffness brought on by travel. Of course, being Madigan, he pushed himself far beyond the limits he needed to but he was *damned* if he would give in to pain.

But, as mentioned, he was mighty glad to cross the bridge for Ciudad Juárez into El Paso and made for the US marshal's office on Creosote Street right away. The deputy marshal on duty was an old friend, Bib Callaghan, and he tugged at his tobacco-stained moustache when he saw Madigan limping into his office.

'Don't tell me – you're totin' more lead!'

Madigan eased himself down into a chair, breathing hard, a little sweat on his face. He folded both hands over the ornately carved handle of the walking-stick.

'No lead in me now,' he said and saw Callaghan frown. 'Yeah, yeah, I know my voice is different.' He tugged down the sweaty blue neckerchief he wore and revealed the edge of the reddened scar. 'Lucky I can talk at all.'

'Well. You never did say much.' Callaghan poured two whiskies from a bottle kept in the bottom of a filing-cabinet and they drank.

'Someone waitin' to see you. Out at Fort Bliss.'

Madigan frowned. 'Don't tell me the damn army is going to jump on me for crossing into Mexico without proper paperwork!'

Bib Callaghan, a man about Madigan's age, but lean as a rail and with more grey in his hair, shook his head. 'Ain't the army wants you. It's Parminter.'

Madigan spluttered as he downed the last of the whiskey. It brought on a fit of coughing that filled his eyes with tears and he held out the glass for a refill. He sipped cautiously when the coughing stopped.

'The hell is he doing down here? He ain't left Washington in years. Five at least that I know of for sure.'

'More like nine or ten. Whatever you sent him in that message must've been dynamite. He's been waitin' two full days for you to arrive.'

Madigan blew out his cheeks. Parminter was one of those men who expected everything to be done yesterday. He had no patience for excuses of delay, hated waiting *any* length of time for a chore to be done or an appointment to be kept. And here he had spent *two days* in a place like El Paso – which he had vocally despised on many an occasion – waiting for Madigan.

'Didn't seem like much, Bib. Caught up with Cadey and he died of wounds, but mistook me for a priest and made a confession before he cashed in his chips. Mostly it had to do with a feller named Mathias Griffin still being alive. Claimed to've shared a cell with him, but dunno when – or where.'

Callaghan took out a pipe and filled the well-broken-in bowl with tobacco and the office with clouds of aromatic smoke before answering.

'You joined the Marshals' Service when, Bronco?'

'Ten years ago come August.'

The other lawman nodded. 'You just missed it then.'

'Missed what?'

'One of Parminter's last jobs in the field. Trackin' down Griffin after the son of a bitch slaughtered a family in north Texas. Got some of his gang – Cadey wasn't one, by the by – and he missed Griffin, even though he looked on and off for years. Then we heard that Griffin had been torn to shreds by a grizzly in Wyoming.' He paused and looked steadily at Madigan. 'That was one other time Parminter left Washington. Went to the place in Wyoming and had the remains exhumed and examined. Still couldn't be certain sure it was Griffin, but he had to be satisfied with what they had and Griffin was never heard of again. That case really got to Parminter, Bronco.'

'Hell, I'd never heard about that.'

'Nope. No one talks about it. Parminter would never allow it. Then after a while it was plumb forgotten.'

'Now it's come back to haunt him.'

Callaghan waved the pipe. 'You feel up to it, Bronco, I'd get out to Fort Bliss pronto. Longer the boss has to wait, tougher he's gonna be.'

23

'Didn't know he could be any other way than tough.'

Bib Callaghan looked very sober as he said, 'Wait'll you hear him talk about Amy Ronan.'

'Who's she?'

'It was her family Griffin butchered. She was the sole survivor. Only seven or eight at the time.'

Chief United States Marshal Miles Parminter was a barrel-chested man and with the beefy shoulders and muscular neck always looked much bigger sitting down than standing.

But he looked plenty big enough now as he came across the office made available to him by the Fort Bliss commandant, right hand held out towards Madigan. He flicked his hard eyes to the walking-stick and then the neckerchief which had slipped enough to show part of the scar.

'Cadey went down fighting,' he remarked as they shook hands. He turned abruptly and went to a padded leather chair, leaving Madigan to hobble across to a straightback across the room. 'I suppose Bib has given you some background.'

'A rough outline . . . for a damn rough case.'

'Damned old gossip,' Parminter muttered. 'You know about Griffin, then?'

Madigan shook his head. 'No, I don't know about Griffin. Except he was a *muy malo hombre* and a lot of people breathed a sigh of relief when he was clawed up by that grizzly.'

'Yes. Except it seems he didn't die there.'

'So Cadey says. Dunno how much faith you can put in his story, chief.'

Parminter leaned forward, elbows on his knees, face hard. 'The man was dying. He knew it, wanted to *confess*, for Chrissakes! He mistook you for a *priest* – and you can explain to me how that happened sometime because I'm damned if I can figure it out. But fact remains, he *believed* he was making his confession to a genuine priest. He was scared. He had no reason to lie.'

'I already figured that out. But I dunno the background to the Griffin thing. Or Cadey's part in it.'

Parminter eased back in his chair, took out a long silver-and-leather case and removed a thin cigarillo from it. He tossed another to Madigan and both men lit up.

The chief marshal's face was stony, his eyes narrowed. 'You're in for a treat, Bren.' He never called Madigan by his nickname of Bronco, always "Bren", short for "Brendan". 'Hope you've got a strong stomach.'

Madigan said nothing, puffed on the excellent cigarillo, got as comfortable as he could and waited for Parminter to start speaking.

Ten years ago, Parminter was a very fit, thick-bodied, hard-eyed man. 'Meanest son of a bitch in the Service', they used to say about him. When he went after a law-breaker, he moved hell and earth and anything in between until he had his man. If a few people died along the way that was the price you had to pay for law and order. He truly believed that.

(He saw a lot of his earlier self in Bren Madigan and that was why it was said on the quiet these days that Madigan, if not exactly Parminter's favourite, sure did pull the 'best' jobs – 'best' being 'toughest' in marshal lingo.)

Miles Parminter hated law-breakers with a passion and some said it was because his own father was an outlaw and brought nothing but misery and tragedy to the Parminter family. It was as if young Miles, by joining the law-enforcers, first as a local sheriff's deputy and later in the Texas Rangers and, later still, the Marshals' Service – was trying to make up for the scars left on the remainder of his family by his wild-ass father, who, incidentally, died in a hail of posse lead in a lonely mountain cabin that was literally shot to splinters by the lawmen. Miles had been a member of that posse and claimed he hadn't known it was his father in the cabin, but others said different.

In any case, once he became deputy US marshal he went into the fray with a vengeance and none of his case files were ever marked 'incomplete' or 'unsolved' or 'open'.

Then came the news about Mathias Griffin, a wild-eyed outlaw who had burst upon the South-west with a savage fury that would be remembered as long as Custer's Last Stand. He was an utterly ruthless man, up to his armpits in blood, a man who never left witnesses and so he avoided capture for many a day.

Then he rode into the lonely Ronan ranch in north Texas, not far from Quanah, near the border of the Indian Territory which was where Griffin had his hideout, beyond the reach of any law but federal. Even then, a US marshal needed all the right papers

26

and warrants to go after a wanted man in the Territory.

Miles Parminter was not known for being a stickler for legal formality and it was mooted that he was not above employing the services of a forger (currently serving time in Canyon City penitentiary) to give him the necessary papers needed to show in court so as to ensure a conviction.

Certainly he didn't worry about signed warrants when he was assigned to the Griffin case. It had horrified the entire South-west.

Mathias Griffin was only an average-size man and he had a pleasant enough face with a disarming smile that had opened many a lonely ranch house door. When he left, if there had been a woman in that ranch house – even a child-woman – he left them dead and mutilated, sometimes hanging the children's bodies from a handy tree or on the front gate to the property or even the clothes-line.

He had two insatiable passions: women and money, in no particular order, although it was said that more than once he had missed an opportunity to become rich simply because he preferred to dally a little longer with a woman he found satisfactory. Not that that saved the woman.

He was clever at his bloody work, smart in his planning of robberies. He never rustled cattle, because it was too much hard work: the inevitable shoot-out with ranch hands, the chase by a posse or a lynch-party. If a man survived those things, he had the problem of selling the spoils and there was never enough money in it.

No, Griffin reckoned the only thing worth stealing – apart from a female – was money itself. Not gold – that could be harder to sell for profit than stolen cattle at times – but *money, greenbacks,* all ready to spend. So he targeted banks and express offices and a train if he thought he could get away with it, even a stagecoach on a payroll run. In each case, the dead piled up because Griffin *never* left witnesses.

But he slipped up with the Ronans.

It was like stumbling across a slice of heaven itself when he and his hard men rode into that lonely Ronan spread in the low hills outside of Quanah. One glance at the clothes-line showed it was filled with feminine frippery: blouses, skirts, dresses, frilly pants, camisoles, even a couple of bonnets. Not a sign of muddy male pants or chaps or woollen work-shirts or boots.

'No men, fellers!' Griffin laughed as he spurred his weary mount forward. They had been running for days ahead of a posse after a particularly brutal hold-up of a Wells Fargo express office and they needed food and rest and fresh mounts.

The Ronan corrals were filled with horses and there were vegetable-gardens and chicken-pens.

'We're home, fellers!' Griffin said, whooping as he rode his mount into the ranch yard, followed at a slower pace by his weary men.

Cadey had been wounded in the chest in their last robbery and it was doubtful if he would see out the night but no one offered to help him. He had to follow the others or be left behind. That was Griffin's Law: never leave witnesses, and don't delay for a wounded gang member. Swaying in the saddle, Cadey eased his mount into the ranch yard.

By that time there were screams coming from inside the house and a sobbing girl-child burst out a rear door, running for the shelter of the barn. Mathias Griffin, hatless, shirt torn and exposing his chest which carried long scratches made from raking fingernails, spattered with blood, lurched into the rear doorway, squinting after the little girl. Cadey, trying to dismount and ending up sprawled on the ground, saw the child's blonde hair streaming behind her, glimpsed her white, terrified face as she looked over her shoulder, tears streaming. He groaned because she reminded him of his kid sister, so long ago, in another world, almost.

Griffin laughed. 'Hey! Beauty! Don't run away from good ol' Uncle Mathias! Your ma's been re-aaal sweet to me and your aunts are pleasin' my men. You come back here and Uncle Mathias'll give you some strap-candy!'

The little girl screamed, stumbled and fell sprawling. Griffin laughed and ran to stand over her as she struggled to get to her feet. He took a handful of that wheat-coloured hair and pulled her half upright. Then little Amy Ronan reached with her small hands into his unbuttoned trousers and squeezed and twisted as hard as she could, driven wild by sheer terror. . . .

Griffin roared and flung her from him, falling to his knees, clawing at himself, face contorted with pain. He vomited, and by that time Amy Ronan was up and running, staggering, screaming. Cadey watched in undisguised horror as he saw Griffin draw

29

his sixgun, hold it in both hands, and begin shooting at the child. He knew whether he lived or died this night, it would be his last with the gang. Griffin had sickened him many a time in the past, but to cold-bloodedly shoot down a little girl like that. . . .

Cadey shook his head, cursing Griffin, looking beyond the man to where the child's body sprawled face down in the dirt. Griffin staggered across, doubled over, smoking gun in hand, and spat on her. Then, still doubled-up, he turned and lurched back towards the house where the screaming had now become one ceaseless chilling wail of terror.

Afterwards, Griffin burned the house with the bodies inside, although for some reason he left the child in the yard *'Let the coyotes pick over her!'* he growled and the gang rode out, leaving Cadey to die where he lay.

Parminter's face was white and strained as he paused in his telling of the attack. He looked at the stub of his cigarillo, flung it away and rubbed a hand across his face.

'Cadey lived, as you know,' he said. 'Don't ask me how. But Amy Ronan owes her life to him, too. She was still alive. Griffin's bullet had hit her high in the leg, almost tore if off. Cadey stopped the bleeding and got her to a swing station just this side of the Territory line. Said she was his daughter and they'd been robbed by outlaws and after he was doctored and recovered some, he just disappeared before any lawmen arrived. Amy eventually got better but that's another story.

30

'I was the lawman they sent to that swing station and I went after Cadey, figuring he would be my link to the rest of the gang. They'd deserted him and I reckoned he'd spill the beans about their hideout.'

Parminter paused, sighed heavily, and took out another cigarillo and lit up. 'I worked on the case for over a year. Never caught up with Cadey but I got me a couple of leads and tracked down Griffin's gang one by one.' He flicked his eyes to the silent Madigan.

'You bring 'em in?'

'From the Territory? I'd have been killed before I rode a mile trying to bring a prisoner out of that country.'

'So they – died.'

'Executed,' Parminter said flatly. 'I'd seen what was left of those Ronan women. Then I got word that Griffin had been torn apart by a grizzly near Laramie. They said it was him, anyway. I guess Bib told you I made 'em dig up what was left. Like leftovers from a wolf pack. How anyone could say for sure it was Griffin . . . well, I had to take their word, but it never did set right – Griffin wasn't the kind of snake to get himself caught in a situation like that, but . . .' He shrugged, spread his hands. 'For the record, he was dead and the case was closed.'

'What about Cadey?'

'Oh, he was caught for some robbery up in Colorado and went to jail. I got to see him and he told me about the Ronan thing and more or less said that, like me, he'd prefer to see Griffin's corpse in an identifiable state. He escaped after that but got picked up in Arizona and spent time in Yuma.

31

Conned his way into parole there and later he was recognized by a sheriff in Socorro as being wanted for escaping Canyon City pen. They threw him in the local jail but he got his hands on a gun and somehow escaped again. Until you ran him down after the train robbery. So, far as we knew, that wiped out the last of Griffin's gang.'

'Except for Griffin himself – if you believe Cadey.'

Parminter's narrowed gaze searched Madigan's face.

'I *have* to believe him, Bren. Don't you see that?'

Madigan saw, all right. Parminter had always prided himself on being the only man in the service never to have left an outstanding file or unsolved case. Now it looked like the biggest case of all in Parminter's book was still wide open.

3
Briefing

'I'm going to indulge myself, Bren,' Parminter said, lounging now in the big padded chair, fingers interlocked across his midriff. His hard eyes just dared Madigan to give him an argument. 'As you know, I don't like failure, can't tolerate it in other people and *won't* tolerate it in myself. For ten years I felt, deep down, that I had failed on that Griffin/Ronan affair. Oh, I told myself over and over, it had to be finished, that Griffin had died in that grizzly's embrace. In fact, I liked to think of him suffering that way, being torn apart and eaten alive. Bloodthirsty, sure, but it would be a fitting end for a monster like Griffin.'

'That's what Cadey called him – a monster. He said "the monster's coming out". And he couldn't die without leaving word for you.'

'Cadey did his share of bloody murder with Griffin,' the chief marshal said curtly. 'It sickened him in the end, he told me that when I saw him in Canyon City prison. And I believed him. Which is also why I believe his "confession" to you. But what we have to do is find out where Griffin is and what name he's using.'

Madigan nodded. 'Cadey said he shared a cell with him. Sounds to me like Griffin's in jail under another name and is either due for release or he's planning to escape. "*The monster's coming out...*" remember. . . .'

Parminter agreed. 'Cadey has been in many prisons so I'd suggest you start by checking them out.' He gestured to a big mahogany desk in one corner. 'I brought all the relevant files with me. You'll find them stuffed into the drawers of that desk. Make a list of prisons Cadey has been in during the last ten years and then fire off a batch of telegraph messages and ask for a list of the other prisoners who shared a cell with him. Any problems, refer them to me.'

'And you'll be where? Back in Washington?'

'Like hell I will! I'll be right here in Fort Bliss, using every facility the army can offer. This is a federal case, Bren, and they're duty-bound to help out. If we need men for a manhunt, I have authority to call on their soldiers, too.'

Madigan mentally blew out his cheeks: By God, the chief was going all out on this, that was for sure!

'Gonna cost a heap one way and another, chief.'

Parminter's face was still set in severe lines. His eyes narrowed characteristically when he was about to say something that brooked no argument.

'This is a legitimate investigation and funds *will* be made available without protest. If not, I'll pay what's necessary out of my own pocket.'

34

Madigan was stunned by the chief's words.

Then Parminter stood and Madigan had a little struggle to stand also. The chief marshal frowned.

'Wound giving you trouble?'

'Bit stiff, is all.'

'Good.' Parminter showed no further interest, but opened the top desk-drawer and dumped a thick cardboard-covered file on the top. He ripped it open, snapping the string that had bound the covers.

'Now. Let's get started.'

Two weeks later, after telegraph messages burned the wires all over the south-west and as far north as the Dakotas, the marshals still didn't know for sure which man Cadey was referring to when he said he had shared a cell with Griffin.

'Cadey's been in and out of jail like a buck jackrabbit at mating time,' Madigan opined, rubbing at his thigh wound absently. It was still sore and stiff but was healing well and although he limped, he could get around easily enough now without the aid of a walking-stick.

'He was damn good at escaping, I'll grant you that,' said Parminter. He was exhibiting his classic signs of impatience at the slowness of results but was holding himself in because he *knew* Madigan was doing all he could at this stage of the investigation. Now he slammed a fist into his palm and seemed to throw himself into an about face, striding across the office he still used in Fort Bliss. 'I've started checks and should see some results by tomorrow or the next day – or I'll know the reason why.' He pulled his

35

mouth into a bitter line. 'Western Union's shares are going to go through the roof before we've finished, Bren.'

'Sometimes get better results talking to a local lawman face to face.'

'Yes, yes, I know. But it's *time*, Bren, *time*, man! If Griffin is about to be released under another name or is planning an escape – hell's teeth, for all we know he might *already* be on the loose!'

Madigan watched his boss, thinking he had never seen him like this. And it suddenly struck him.

'The girl – Amy Ronan. You figure she could be still in danger?'

Parminter stopped in mid-stride and the sharp look that came Madigan's way should have impaled him. Then the chief marshal drew down a deep breath and made himself calmly take a cigarillo from his case and go through the motions of lighting up.

'It's possible. She's eighteen, going on nineteen now, and quite good looking, so I hear. She ended up with one leg a little shorter than the other, thanks to Griffin's bullet.' His voice had softened.

'I heard a few years back that she was leading a more or less normal life, had finished schooling and found herself a job.' Then his face drew into tight lines. 'Can you imagine, have you any concept of the utter *terror* that girl must have gone through that day at her mother's ranch? Eight years old and Griffin's gang doing their bloody work on her mother and aunts. Then that blood-splattered bastard turning on her . . . it's a wonder her heart didn't stop!'

'She sounded pretty damn gutsy from what Cadey

36

said, grabbing Griffin that way.'

'Damn right! And had her leg almost blow off in return! Bren, I know Griffin better than most. I made sure I found out everything I could before I went after him . . . He was well known for molesting young girls and – well, I've always had the feeling that sooner or later it was going to bother him that Amy Ronin had not only foiled his intentions that day but was still alive somewhere. He's been on the run, having to stay undercover because he's supposed to be dead. But now he's seen Cadey again and in my opinion that would've brought it all back to him. And he's such a sick son of a bitch that I'm afraid that with his warped mind he's going to start thinking again about Amy Ronan and wondering how she looks now she's a near-grown woman . . . ripe for the picking.'

Madigan frowned. *Hell, the Old Man had it bad!* Aloud, he asked, 'Is Griffin that loco?'

'Worse! Far worse! No one can get inside that twisted mind of his. But I've tried, had expert help, and I still believe he will go after her.'

'But he won't know where she is, will he? In fact, do *we* know where she is?'

Parminter hesitated. 'That's your job. Find her, tell her what's happened, and give her any protection she needs. Meantime, I'll keep trying to track down which prison Cadey could've met Griffin in.'

Madigan handed him a paper. 'I've made a list of Cadey's cell-mates. Some have died – I put a cross beside their names – some have been released, and others are still doing hard time.'

Parminter scanned the list, nodding gently to himself. 'And they could be planning a break-out. Nothing to lose if they're doing life.'

'I have a feeling that it wasn't all that long before Cadey died that he ran into Griffin,' Madigan added. 'Just a hunch.'

Parminter knew his top marshal well enough to accept Madigan's hunches. He nodded. 'All right. I'll start working back from the bottom of the list. Although I reckon I can cross out the last one.'

'Why?'

'Because it's the local jail in Socorro. Not likely to find Griffin in one of those small-town jails, not with a record like he's got.'

'But he was using another name, boss. Only Cadey knew he was really Griffin.'

Parminter snapped his head up, frowned, pursed his lips. 'Ye-es – that's a damn good point, Bren. I'll make the first wire to the Socorro sheriff. Meantime, you find Amy.'

That was as straight an order as Madigan had ever been given: not *try* – just *do* it. No excuses. . . .

'Where do I start?' he asked.

'I lost track of her after she left school in St Louis. Heard she was headed for a job in Albuquerque.'

'Not much to go on!'

Parminter's brittle eyes fixed on Madigan's face. 'I don't *have* any other information, so – start there. *Now!*'

The prison was called Flogging Creek penitentiary, although the 'creek' had been dry for years. Inmates called it Satan's Dungeon, because most prisoners never lived long enough to serve out their sentences and the next stop just had to be Hell itself.

And no one serving time in that prison figured Hell could be worse than the pen.

The prison stood in the middle of an arid plain, an island of grey and brown stone, walls ten feet high and topped with rolls of barbed wire, look-out stations at every corner and wooden towers inside the walls to cover every inch of the iron-hard bare ground. Prisoners slept shackled on long wooden benches in airless dormitories below ground level. No matter what, the chains were *never* unlocked during the night. The manacles went on at sundown and stayed there till sun-up. A man could die during the dark hours but his body wouldn't be removed before the first hint of grey tinged the bleak hills at the edge of the plain.

The prison had been built ten years ago and in all that time, no one had escaped, no one had even successfully broken out of their cells or dorms, let alone reached the outside. No – when a man was sentenced to life in Flogging Creek penitentiary, they really meant sentenced to *death*.

But there was one man – a man who called himself Matt Mayfield, the likes of whom no one at the prison – guard, warden or other prisoners, had ever seen.

'Goddamn walls won't hold me,' Mayfield had said, quite cheerfully and confidently, when he had first arrived a few weeks previously. His easy-going, somewhat disarming smile showed through all the filth and beard-shag as the others scoffed at his boast.

The big bald man called Skull thrust his beer-keg belly towards the smaller Mayfield, who was only an average-size man, possibly in his late thirties but he looked younger. Unless you looked deep into his eyes – then you decided he was ageless, because those eyes were fathomless, like looking into the blackest pool in the middle of the darkest swamp.

But that kind of thing didn't bother Skull. He'd never yet met a man he couldn't kill within seconds if the notion took him.

'You'll die here like the rest of us!' Skull told Mayfield, whose grin widened.

'I'll send you a postcard from New Orleans, Skull. Picture of them French dancers doin' the can-can – and it's the real thing. They don't wear no pants.'

Skull curled a thick lip. He poked a heavy finger into Mayfield's chest, the power of the casual thrust causing Mayfield to step back so as to keep balance.

'You'll *die* here, I said!' Skull growled. 'An' mebbe sooner than you think, you keep sassin' me!'

Mayfield put up both hands in front of him. 'Take it easy, *amigo*. Didn't mean no harm. . . .' He looked around at the ugly faces standing in the semicircle while they waited for the guards to come and put on the shackles for the night. 'Thought all you men might enjoy the postcard. I've seen that dance in the French quarter of N'Orleans, and I'm here to tell you. . . .'

Then the guards came in and in the general shuffling around, Mayfield managed to get himself next to a short man with a thick chest. The man looked mighty worried all the time. His name was Kimborough and he was doing life for beheading his own mother; a contrite, fearful man.

Mayfield nodded to him in friendly manner while he awaited the shackles.

'Matt Mayfield. They call you "Kim", right?'

Kimborough looked at him with his worried eyes and after a time nodded slowly.

'OK, Kim.' Mayfield dropped his voice now as the guards worked their way down the line with chains and manacles, two back-up men carrying shotguns and with nail-studded billies swinging from their belts. 'Hear tell you're an engineer.'

Kimborough's lined face remained frozen, his eyes blank, but after the guards had shackled them and moved across to the next row, he said hoarsely, 'I'm – I'm a filthy murderer! I killed my own mother!'

'Kim,' Mayfield said easily in friendly tones, 'that don't count for much in here.'

'Well, what're you in for?'

Mayfield's face straightened briefly, but then the friendly smile came back. 'A woman claimed I beat her up and tried to – well work her over with a knife. *Then* the bitch said I'd told her how I'd cut up another woman in Tucson . . .'

'Did you?'

Mayfield laughed but there was little mirth in the sound. He poked Kimborough hard in the ribs, making him gasp.

'Kim, *amigo*, you just don't ask them sorta questions. Liable to get you killed. But, don't worry. I'll look after you in here. What sort of engineer were you?'

Kimborough could hardly breathe and he squirmed as far away from Mayfield as he could, gasping, 'I drove tunnels for a mining company.'

Mayfield laughed shortly. 'Just what I wanted to hear, *amigo. Exactly* what I wanted to hear.'

4
Break-Out

They decided that as Socorro was on the way to Albuquerque Madigan should stop off and see Sheriff Tate McGill. Madigan had travelled by stage and would continue on to Albuquerque by train after he had spoken with McGill.

The sheriff showed him no real welcome: like a lot of local lawmen in the West, he was always suspicious when a federal marshal appeared, expecting criticism of the way he was doing his job, or, if the lawman had been involved in a little graft or corruption to help supplement his meagre pay, then the cold sweat broke out.

Tate McGill's handshake was brief and without much warmth, but he nodded several times as he sat down at his desk in his office. He didn't offer Madigan a chair but the marshal took the only one spare and hooked one heel over his left knee as he thumbed back his hat and took out tobacco-sack and papers.

'You're a long way from home, Marshal,' the sheriff said finally after a long uncomfortable wait while Madigan built his cigarette and lit up.

'Usually am. Or, looking at it another way, home is where I happen to be come sundown.'

McGill didn't seem as if he was quite sure what to make of that. He scratched his long nose and ran a hand through long, lank hair, looping some greasy strands behind one ear.

'Yeah? Not an outdoor man myself. Now what you want?'

'Co-operation. Yours.'

The sheriff shrugged non-committally.

'Let me look at your arrest records for the past three months.'

McGill didn't like that and seemed as if he would give Madigan some kind of argument but changed his mind when those hard eyes bored into him like a couple of steel rods. He sighed as he heaved up a thick, dog-eared ledger from the floor on his side of the desk. He blew dust off the cover and opened the book two-thirds of the way through. He started to read it, lips moving, murmuring in such a way that Madigan couldn't make out a thing the man was saying. So he reached across the desk and took the book, earning a cold, narrow look from McGill.

'I asked to see it, not have it read to me.'

McGill scowled, filled a pipe while Madigan read down swiftly.

'What made you arrest Cadey?'

The sheriff frowned through a cloud of smoke. 'Cadey? Oh, yeah. He came in lookin' like a saddle tramp, but within an hour was all spruced up and havin' his way with two of the local whores – throwin' money around like he had the key to the First National Bank's vault.'

'Fair enough,' Madigan allowed. 'And you tossed him in the cells while you looked into whatever story he gave you, huh?'

'Yeah. Tried to tell me he—'

'Not interested,' the marshal broke in rudely. 'You put him in a cell with a feller name of . . .' He looked at the book again. 'Matt Mayfield?' When the offended-looking McGill nodded, Madigan said, 'Tell me about Mayfield.'

The sheriff frowned. 'You sure are a damn grasshopper, ain't you?' Madigan waited patiently. 'Well, Mayfield beat up on a whore and as he'd busted her nose and spoiled her looks, I figured a couple weeks on the local chain-gang would teach the sonuver a lesson. But the whore, when she found out she wasn't gonna look so pretty even when her nose was healed, claimed he tried to cut her with a knife and that when he was drunk he'd boasted how he'd carved up some woman in Tucson.'

He had Madigan's attention now, the marshal leaning forward in his chair, elbows on his knees. McGill began to feel a little more important.

'Well, so happened I'd been bonin' up some of the dodgers and messages that'd come in and I'd read about a woman in Tucson bein' found all chopped up, stuffed into a grain-bin in a shed behind some stables.' He puffed at his pipe and his chest seemed to swell. 'I sent a coupla wires and it nailed down this Mayfield pretty good. He was there at the time, had been seen with the woman. Upshot was he went to trial and got thirty years in Floggin' Creek pen.'

'Which is the same as saying he'll die there behind them stone walls.'

'Sure. And the bastard deserves it, from what I heard he done to that woman.' McGill suddenly snapped his fingers. 'You never come to see about Cadey at all, did you? You're more interested in Mayfield! Well, I'm the one got things movin' and they couldn't've nailed him without me . . .'

'Without the whore who told you about him, you mean. But that makes no nevermind, McGill. I found out what I want to know about Mayfield. . . . Obliged.'

Madigan stood, closed the book and dropped it on to the desk. A cloud of dust rose. McGill coughed.

'There some kinda reward for Mayfield?'

'Dunno. You wouldn't see any of it, anyway. You're just doing your job. One other thing you can help me with: where's the telegraph shack in this town?'

McGill scowled, heaved his legs on to a corner of his desk and crossed his ankles. He gestured vaguely towards the heat-pulsing street outside his door.

'Just turn left along Main. You'll come to it.'

Madigan did – and sent off a priority wire to Marshal Parminter.

He was just paying the telegraph agent for his ticket to Albuquerque when the telegraph man came running down to the depot, waving a yellow message-form.

'Just come in for you,' he panted. Madigan took the form quickly.

It was from Parminter.

MAYFIELD'S OUR MAN. HE JUST MADE HISTORY BY BEING THE FIRST EVER TO ESCAPE FROM FLOGGING CREEK. GET TO ALBUQUERQUE SOONEST. MILES PARMINTER.

'But you can't tunnel under those walls! The foundations either go too deep or they're resting on bedrock!'

Kimborough was emphatic, showing some kind of emotion other than anxiety for the first time since Mayfield's arrival. Matt Mayfield grinned and clapped Kimborough lightly on the shoulder. They were in a corner of the yard, supposed to be stacking cords of firewood, but Mayfield had insisted they take a breather. Now that Kimborough had said his piece he began to take on that worried look again, head swinging, searching for any patrolling guard; he went white, even came close to throwing up, just at the mention of the flogging post – and ten lashes was the penalty for loafing on the job.

'We – we better get back.'

'Relax, Kim!' Mayfield seemed to make light of everything but Kimborough was astute enough to see behind the façade of comradeship, knowing he was being used – but not caring much, anyway.

He deserved to be punished for what he had done and only wished the judge had sentenced him to the gallows instead of this lingering hell in here.

'Kim, I ain't talkin' about goin' *under* the walls. We're goin' *through.*'

Kimborough's jaw dropped. 'You – you're crazy! It'd take dynamite!'

Mayfield's smile tightened some. 'Now we're pards, Kim, but you go easy on that "crazy" talk – Okay? Listen, I said we're goin' through and that's what we're gonna do. You reckon we could dig a short tunnel from, say, the washroom, into the big drain where they empty the bathin' kegs?'

Kimborough blinked, stared, getting his mind working on the question, picturing the draughty wooden wash-house where once a week the water-tankers brought refills for the large kegs used by the prisoners for bathing. Ten men, one after the other, used the keg; the last man in came out almost as dirty as before he'd stepped into the filthy armpit-deep water. Then it was emptied into a stone-lined trough that ran into a network of drains passing beneath the quadrangle. It exited outside the walls into an eroded gully, flooding out through slimy iron bars across the end of the four-foot-diameter pipe. A lot of water came from twenty-five kegs. . . .

'Ye-es, that's possible,' Kim conceded.

Mayfield's grin widened. 'Okay! We'll be outa here in a couple of weeks. Think about that!'

Kim didn't believe but he found his mind wrestling with the details of the tunnel just the same; the scrap timber to shore up the walls, the digging-tools, then, breaking through the stone-lined walls into the drainage system. . . .

It kept him so busy he had to be spoken to several

times before he answered and earned himself several brutal cuffs from the guards for day-dreaming.

But, by Godfrey, Mayfield was right: they could do it in a couple of weeks.

Actually, it took seventeen days, with seven men working in shifts. How Mayfield arranged this, Kimborough never knew, but he took Skull into his confidence and the big man chose five others, dangerous types with nothing to lose if they were caught, everything to gain if the plan worked.

But the day they were to break through into the drainage system, Mayfield wasn't with them. He was in writhing pain and a semi-coma in the prison infirmary, under the casual care of old Doc Swanston, or Soaker as he was known amongst both prisoners and guards. He was a drunk and couldn't have possibly earned a living as a doctor in the outside world. But the prisons department of Arizona employed him because he was cheap, and the law said they needed a medic on staff. And Doc Swanston was happy, because he could get free booze from the warden by passing on scraps of information his patients told him in confidence or let slip while under chloroform or in a coma.

Mayfield was in his sick-bed simply because he wanted to be.

There was no way he could have gotten out of the dormitory at night, so, during his working day, he managed to break two amber-and-red splotched leaves off a croton-bush growing at the edge of the warden's garden. In bed that night, he chewed half a leaf, hoping it would be enough.

It was. Within hours he was groaning in pain, his bowels voiding where he lay, vomiting, earning the curses of those near him, because no guards would come before morning to clean up the mess or attend to him.

Skull said in a hoarse whisper, 'Tomorrow's the day, Mayfield! We're goin' whether you're there or not!'

'Wait – wait up – just one day – I – I'll be okay by then!' Mayfield gasped but Skull just laughed.

'Tomorrow! Has to be. You said you'd fixed it with the guard to unlock them bars for tomorrow so we're goin'.'

Mayfield was too sick to argue and when he was finally taken to the infirmary he seemed to be nearly unconscious. He felt mighty bad but not as bad as he had made out and he was glad he hadn't chewed a whole damn leaf! He felt scoured out, his head spinning, ears ringing. Once abed, the muttering sawbones pottered about, giving him stomach powders and lotions, even considering bleeding a pint of blood from the ailing man.

But Mayfield rolled his eyes and thrashed around, speaking in slurred tones, and it was a little while before the doctor paid close attention.

'Fools. They'll never make it! . . . Tunnel's startin' to cave in already – by tomorrow with the weight of them water-wagons passin' over it tonight – it'll fall in on 'em . . .'

Suddenly, Doc Swanston's clawed hand shook Mayfield's shoulder and he made a pretence of focusing his eyes.

'What're you talking about, mister?' the medic whispered hoarsely, leaning close, his sickening breath making Mayfield's belly somersault. 'Tunnels – cave-ins – someone trying to dig their way out . . .? C'mon! Tell me!'

He shook Mayfield roughly and the prisoner groaned, knowing the doctor was thinking of how much booze he could hit the warden for if he gave him information about an attempted break-out.

Mayfield moaned, getting a plea into his voice.

'Don't – get – rough! I'm sick . . .'

'Mister, I can make you a whole lot *sicker* if I want! Now you tell me about this tunnel!'

Mayfield made himself look afraid, wild-eyed. In a few gasping, stumbling sentences, he told the whole escape plan and Swanston grinned, showing his yellowed teeth.

'When they gonna do it?'

'Mornin' – early – mornin' . . .'

The medic patted Mayfield's shoulder lightly. He was the only patient because a man had to be near death to qualify for time off in the infirmary. 'You're a good boy. I'll get you better for this. But first I gotta go see the warden.'

'Aw, no!' grated Mayfield, looking upset. 'I never meant for you to tell . . .'

'You stay put! I'll be back!'

The stooped old man hurried out. Actually, he was only in his early fifties but alcohol had added years to his looks and the way he moved.

As soon as he was gone, Mayfield got out of bed, alarmed at how groggy he felt and how weak his knees were. But he overcame the feeling, went to the drawer where Swanston kept his instruments, made his selection, then went back to bed.

During the night he called for help, screaming that he was in terrible pain. No one came and Mayfield grinned. The doc would be deep in an alcoholic stupor by now and wouldn't wake until well into the morning. By that time, Mayfield planned to be a long way from the prison.

The warden was never a man to pass up a chance to make more suffering for his charges and after organizing his men to ambush the intended escapees, he rounded up dormitories K and D and had the men gather in the wash-house. They milled about, bewildered and suspicious. The hard-faced warden never addressed the prisoners directly, so his deputy told them that this week they were having *two* baths – but they had to be finished in one hour, all eighty men, and then they would empty the twenty-five barrels of filthy, lye-smelling water down the drains – upon his signal and not before.

In the tunnel, Skull and a mighty nervous Kimborough and the others crawled in through the narrow space they had dug, scraping against the splintery shoring timbers. Skull led the way and when he came to the dirt wall at the end, set his stub of candle down and scraped at the thin layer with horny hands, revealing the stonework of the drain wall.

They passed up the short length of log that Mayfield had stolen from the firewood pile and Skull made them back up while he swung against the stones. It took several hard blows before the first stone moved, creaking, and then it slid out of its place and clattered into the drain beyond. A little daylight seeped in and the prisoners pressed forward eagerly as Skull cursed them, battered other rocks free until the hole was wide enough for him to squeeze through.

One by one they gathered in the slimy stinking drain and, coughing, they made their way around the bend towards the source of the daylight. It was a bright morning and the iron bars across the drain's exit into the gully were sharply silhouetted. Skull waded through the knee-deep filth, crouched double because of the narrowness of the drain. He was gasping in anticipation now, hoping that Mayfield had paid off the guard who was supposed to unlock the bars so they could swing out and give the prisoners their freedom. *Too bad about Mayfield*, he chuckled to himself as his big hands gripped the slippery, rust-pitted metal. He pushed. He slipped with his effort, banging his face against the iron. Swearing, he tried again, slid to his knees.

'Oh, dear God!' wailed out Kimborough. 'We're trapped!'

'Pull instead of pushin'!' rasped one of the others and Skull tried but the iron bars were locked solid, unmoving. . . .

'What the hell! Mayfield *told* me he had it all fixed,' he growled.

'What the hell's *that?*' croaked one of the men and they all heard it then: the gathering rumbling roar, they felt the pipe trembling beneath their feet, the pressure of air compressed ahead of a raging wall of water.

One by one they began to scream as they realized they were about to drown.

Only a few feet above them, the empty water-wagons rumbled through the gates of the prison stockade, the large wooden-slatted tanks steaming a little in the hot morning sun as it dried out their moisture.

Inside the second of the three wagons, Matt Mayfield strained with hands and feet against the slippery staves of the tank, the few gallons of cold water remaining in the bottom sloshing over him to the waist. It was damned uncomfortable and he would be a mass of bruises by the time they reached the railroad tanks outside of town where they would refill.

But he laughed anyway, the sound booming back at him from the rounded walls. It was dark in here but there was plenty of air for him to breathe. He laughed again, thinking of those seven men in the tunnel, and what the warden would do to them.

He didn't yet know that the warden had ordered the emptying of the water-kegs into the drainage system while the men were trapped up against the iron bars. Mayfield hadn't even approached a guard about unlocking them. For he had never intended to try to escape via the tunnel. That was just a diversion while he found his own way to freedom.

The doctor wouldn't come out of his boozy sleep until about now. He would panic when he found Mayfield wasn't in his bed but he would search and delay telling the warden for at least another hour, likely more. And, in any case, the warden would be so busy clearing up whatever mess was left at the tunnel and having his deputy explain to the assembled inmates that he had just proved once more that there was absolutely *no* way to escape from Satan's Dungeon, that he wouldn't be interested in anything else for a time.

Then, finally, when Doc Swanston got up enough courage to tell him Matt Mayfield was missing. . . .

He laughed again, knowing the sound would be drowned out by the rumbling of the empty wagon as the weary team dragged the heavy tanks behind them across the burning plains.

It had been easy getting into the empty tanks last night: they were standing free, the teams bedded down in the stables with good grain and oats for the night. There was a guard, but he was asleep: no one had ever attempted to get into the empty wagons before.

He was still sleeping, and would sleep for ever. Mayfield had seen to that with the precise placement of the sharpened probe he had taken from the infirmary at the base of the skull. There was no blood, or what little had oozed from the small hole would have been covered by the man's tunic collar. They would think he had died in his sleep.

That's if they even bothered to look; most interest would be focused on the tunnel and the escape attempt.

When the tankers finally arrived at the railroad siding outside of town, they were left standing in the sun near the huge metal water-tanks raised on pilings while the drivers walked on into the depot for coffee and their breakfast. Refilling would take place afterwards.

Mayfield turned the locking bar on the round filling-cap on top of the tank and eased it aside. He had to struggle to get his shoulders through but he made it, unseen, and dropped to the ground, sprawling on all fours.

'Judas priest! Where the hell'd you come from!'

The voice startled Mayfield and he spun towards the sound, glimpsing the unexpected guard clawing at his holstered pistol. Mayfield's right hand went beneath his ragged jacket and something glittered in the sunlight as the razor-sharp scalpel sliced into the man's throat. He clawed at himself, blood spurting, legs folding. Mayfield slashed him twice more, kicked the body away from him and hastily removed the trousers and boots – and sixgun rig – out of sight behind the front pilings of the water-tanks above. The shirt was too cut up and bloody to wear, but he found the man's horse in a shady depression and there was a spare in the saddle-bags.

He was singing to himself after hiding the guard inside the empty tank that he had ridden into town; he chuckled as he made his way back to the horse which had a warbag and a sheathed rifle attached to the saddle rig.

He swung aboard a little stiffly and rode away into the heat haze.

Now he was free again, *tasting* it in the hot air, feeling it swell his breast, setting his blood pumping. Free to roam and do what he wanted.

56

He made himself a promise that he would take the first woman he saw, young or old or anywhere in between, even if he had to kill whoever she was with.

Yeah! He liked setting himself that kind of chore! The danger only added to the good feeling he knew he would get once he had her alone in some remote place where she could scream her terror until her heart burst and no one would hear.

No one but him.

It was time now to kill off 'Matthew Mayfield'. The name had been useful enough these past few years but now he had been linked to that woman's murder in Arizona it was pointless to keep using it. Might as well revert to his real name – he didn't care any longer how many lawmen were after him. Come to think of it, he had *never* cared about that. The more who came, the more he killed.

But now, this was going to be a special time. Running into good old Cadey in that hick jail had been a real stroke of luck – something that was *meant* to be, in his book.

Cadey had been scared when he'd realized who his cellmate was and had talked a hell of a lot to cover up. He'd said more than he'd meant to, admitted he'd been the one to save the kid. *No wonder he'd had a gun smuggled in and had high-tailed it without inviting his old pard along. Son of a bitch!*

He had stirred old memories, *good* old memories – and had brought to the fore a hard-to-shake frustration that had kept him awake nights on and off over the years, after he'd learned the kid had survived. *The little whelp!*

The way she'd fought him that long-ago day, near crippled him, and he had shot her, sure a single .45 slug would have killed a damn eight-year-old snotty-nosed brat. But he had been drunk, on blood and booze, too drunk to realize she might still be alive.

It had hacked him for years, knowing she was out there, somewhere, out of his reach, and then, along came Cadey and let slip that he knew where she was – or had been. *Trying to make amends, even though the gang had run out on him.*

Well, *he* knew now, and he already itched to see her face when once again she looked into the eyes of her worst nightmare.

Mathias Griffin.

5
The Hunter

Madigan had always like Albuquerque. He liked the way it sprawled out, with plenty of space between the adobe buildings, though there were a lot more clapboard-and-frame houses going up now that the railroad had arrived.

In his pocket, as he walked slowly up towards the main plaza, shouldering his war bag with his rifle slid under the straps in its leather scabbard, were two more wires from Parminter. One was to the effect that there was now some possibility that Cadey and his gang had had inside information about the payroll train they had robbed. There were still at least two known members of the gang on the loose and Madigan was to go after these, but only after he had ensured the safety of Amy Ronan.

The second wire told him that Amy had graduated in bookkeeping and accountancy and had showed a lot of interest in pottery-making as a hobby. Albuquerque seemed a likely place to start the search, then, in Madigan's book, because there was a lot of traditional Indian and Mexican-style pottery made in the town and surrounding district.

He was well aware that there were members of Cadey's gang still on the loose – Shell Markham and Zac Berry, he knew of for sure. They were rough-tough *hombres*, killers when they had to be, long-time outlaws and used to living wild. It had been while trying to track them that he had stumbled across Cadey, the leader of the train robbers.

But to hell with Markham and Berry for now. Finding the girl and making sure she was safe from this sonuver Griffin had to take priority.

He called into the rust-coloured abode post-office and found a third wire waiting for him from Parminter. The chief wasn't kidding when he said Western Union's shares were going to go through the roof! The man was spending money like a drunken cowhand. Not long ago, a marshal had to fill out a form in triplicate to warrant his sending more than one telegraph message a week while on assignment.

The long, wearying train-journey up from Socorro had made Madigan hungry and feeling in need of a bath. So he ate excellent Mexican chilli in a plaza cantina, downed a couple of beers to cool his palate and then located a bath-house where he soaked in hot suds up to his neck for half an hour. His hip felt better, having stiffened up during the train journey, and whenever he could he exercised it, stretching the leg, swinging it to loosen up the joint. But he knew he wouldn't be running any races for a while and he still walked with a limp. The scar on his neck

was mighty noticeable and made him look like a fugitive from a lynching, he thought, but his looks were
the least of his worries. His voice, though, was still
raspy and didn't seem to be improving.

He booked a room at a boarding-house where he
left his war bag and, reluctantly, his rifle, then went
in search of the local law.

Sheriff Blade was a short man, heading into his
sixties, mostly bald, with tufts of silver-grey hair above
his big ears. He had the appearance of a prune-faced
gnome, and one of the deepest voices Madigan had
ever heard coming out of such a small chest. You
could tell that Blade was proud of it, too; he rolled
his words off his tongue precisely, filled the small
office with mellow sound.

'Been expecting you, Marshal. Carried out a small
investigation on your behalf. Sure you'll find it satisfactory.'

The man pushed a small sheaf of papers across the
neat desk and Madigan noticed his hands were soft,
the nails rounded and clean, and there was a gold
signet-ring set with a red stone on the little finger of
his right hand. His clothes were neat, too; clean,
pressed, good quality. He looked more like a lawman
in Washington's suburbs than one out here. Madigan
read the papers – or tried to. It was such an untidy
scrawl that he had to ask several times what the words
were. It made Blade irritable and Madigan somehow
felt glad that he had discovered some flaw in the man.
Obviously it irked Blade not to be able to write neatly.

Madigan snapped his head up. 'This all boils down
to saying Amy Ronan never came to Albuquerque.'

Blade steepled his fingers as he leaned back in his chair. 'As far as I can ascertain. I've only been here a little over a year myself. Elected to the post, mind, not just a gun hiring on for a few dollars.'

It seemed important to Blade that he got that point across. He gestured now to the papers Madigan held.

'I've made a list of the young women who arrived in this town about three years ago, the time you're interested in. Not many. One got married and settled down. Two moved on and the other is now one of the leading ladies-of-the-night at our largest saloon, the Wardance.'

'Good work, Blade. You ought to be a marshal.' Madigan knew at once he shouldn't have said that: Blade would never have passed the entrance, because of his height – or lack of it – and his face now hardened into rocklike lines, his eyes hooding.

'I have always felt that I could offer some useful talents to the Marshal Service, Madigan, but I am content in my present job. And I am pleased that you consider my investigative work up to your no doubt exacting standards.'

There was a touch of bitterness and a lot of sarcasm in that last and Madigan stood, rubbing his thigh as he nodded, thanking the man before leaving with the list. Blade watched him go, mouth tight.

'Big arrogant bastard!' he said, the words booming around the small office.

The women on Blade's list checked out exactly as he had written about them. Leastways, they all did until

62

Madigan came to the one who worked in the railroad depot, in the Accounting and Schedules Section. The agent was helpful enough, pointed her out in the surprisingly crowded depot office where four women worked at small desks.

'Lot of rail traffic passes through here,' the agent explained, 'as you no doubt have worked out for yourself. I mean, just take a look at our assembly yards . . .' He waved a hand towards the network of tracks shining like silver wire in the sun that blazed down from a spectacularly blue and cloudless sky. 'I've worked for the railroad in St Louis and I can tell you now that Albuquerque is gonna boom, so if you've got any spare cash you want to invest I can put you on to some good land within a frog's leap of town and—'

'How long has that girl been working here?' interrupted Madigan, nodding towards a young woman at a corner desk, who was using a counting-frame and writing in a notebook. She had brown hair that was parted down the middle and pulled back severely about her head, covering her ears, fixed in a bun at the back. What he could see of her face was pleasant and plain as she concentrated on her work.

'Oh, that's Mary Kirk. She was here when I came out from St Louis to get this show on the road. About a year ago. The town started to fill up with folk around that time when they opened the railroad . . .' He saw Madigan was about to interrupt and said quickly, 'She's in her early twenties, too old for the one you want.'

'Yeah. Know where she came from?'

'Understand she'd worked with the railroad before. My guess is that, like me, she was transferred here. I think she mentioned Denver once. Look, she's in the midst of changing our schedules so if you want to talk with her I'd be obliged if you could leave it for a spell.'

Madigan hesitated, watching the girl. She had lifted her gaze towards him and the agent a couple of times but looked away quickly, making notes in her book with her right hand, working the counters with her left. She looked to be efficient enough.

'Okay. Thanks, Mr Tanner. Might want to talk with the Kirk girl later, but doesn't look as if this Amy Ronan stayed in Albuquerque. No one remembers her so I figure she must've been using another name.'

As he was turning away, the Kirk girl stood and turned to a filing-cabinet close to her desk, went to the top drawer and took out a folder before sitting down again.

Well, that settled it, anyway, Madigan thought. *She doesn't use a walking-stick. . . .*

He crossed her name off the list and left. It was afternoon now and he was hungry again; he went back to the Mexican cantina and had another bowl of chilli, some tortillas, and a jug of beer.

How come folk never recalled a young woman using a walking-stick who arrived about two or three years ago? he asked himself. The name wouldn't be too important, but folk would surely remember a beautiful young girl in her late teens who had to use a walking-stick to get around.

64

Looked like it all came down to wrong information: Amy Ronan never came here in the first place.

So-ooooo – where next?

He went back to see Blade and asked about Markham and Berry.

'Those two outlaws?' the little lawman said, shaking his head. 'They would know better than to show their faces in my bailiwick. They helped rob a train in my jurisdiction and I put out a dead-or-alive dodger on them. They wouldn't want to tangle with me, I assure you.'

Well, nothing like having a good opinion of yourself.

'I need to know something about their stamping-ground. Can you fill me in? And any other info you've got.'

'I've got plenty.' Blade scowled a little. 'Trouble is I seem to have scared them off completely.'

'Seems like it,' Madigan said quietly, trying to keep the sarcasm out of his voice. 'Let's see what you've got.'

Blade hesitated but went to a filing-cabinet which looked to be as neat as everything else, though Madigan would bet it would be like trying to read drunken Chinese writing. Blade handed the file to the marshal.

'I can probably be of assistance to you with those two. In the field, I mean.'

His eyes were steady on Madigan's face as the marshal shook his head. 'It's federal, Blade. Sorry.'

'I would like the opportunity of helping apprehend those two, Marshal. I feel I ought to be in at the kill so to speak.'

'You've done your part. It's my job now. I'll return this file later.'

He left the law-office, sure he heard Blade mutter something uncomplimentary as he did so. To hell with him – Blade wasn't going to climb aboard any glory-wagon using Madigan as a step-up if he could help it.

Madigan strolled through the clear evening of the town and decided to exercise his hip some, so he walked out as far as the railroad depot where lights still burned and a freight train was loading at the siding. He rolled a cigarette, leaned against the depot wall and smoked slowly, watching the activity. He turned his head as a door opened on the far side of the depot building, and glanced through the window which gave a view to the other side through another window there. A woman was leaving, her clothes drab in the dull lantern-light, a bonnet throwing her face into shadow. She appeared to lock the door behind her before turning away and starting back towards town.

She was limping! Throwing her left leg awkwardly out to one side in a kid of jerky semicircle with each step . . .

Madigan straightened, flicking the cigarette away, holding the file under his arm as he hurried around the depot building. By that time, she was half-way to the edge of town.

He had started out to overtake her, but now dropped back, letting her get well ahead. She went into a store and came out carrying a package of some kind and then made her way towards one of the newer frame houses that had been built since the railroad's arrival. It wasn't very big, one, possibly two, bedrooms, single-storeyed, raised on short stumps that were supposed to help keep snakes away as well as making for better air-circulation.

He watched from under a tree as a light appeared in a side window, then another at the rear, likely the kitchen. Soon he smelled food cooking and went to the rear door. As he raised his hand to knock, the woman screamed.

Madigan went in fast, dropping Blade's file, palming up his sixgun.

There were two men and they were stalking the girl: Mary Kirk. She held the skillet with her omelette in one hand, the stirring-fork in the other as she backed away. Her eyes widened when she saw Madigan and she threw the contents of the pan into the face of the nearest man. He screamed, clawing at his eyes. She stabbed him in the arm with the fork, then moved to the table in one lithe motion, over-turning it and plunging the room into semi-darkness as the lamp crashed to the floor. The second man didn't seem able to make up his mind whether to stop the girl going through the doorway into the parlour or to turn on Madigan.

He shouldn't have hesitated. Madigan lunged at him, smashing the gun out of his hand, swinging his own sixgun backhand into the man's face. The attacker grunted, staggered back, face masked in blood, legs buckling. Madigan kicked him in the stomach as he fell writhing, spun when he heard the man with the burned face curse behind him.

There was a gun pointing at him and Madigan

dived to the side as it roared, rattling the walls, it seemed. He triggered at the muzzle-flash while still moving sideways. He fired again and this time the man threw up his arms, slammed back against the wall and clattered to the floor.

Madigan strode through into the parlour and almost had his head blown off as a shotgun thundered and the charge of buckshot chewed a fist-sized chunk out of the doorframe. Splinters stung one side of his face and neck as he threw up an arm instinctively, froze as he heard the second gun-hammer cocking.

'Hold it!' he yelled in his raspy voice, glimpsing the girl crouching over the smoking shotgun, finger tightening on the trigger as she prepared to empty the second barrel into him. 'I'm a US marshal! You must've seen me down at the depot earlier, talking with Mr Tanner.'

Her face was white, mouth tight, nostrils pinched, eye slitted dangerously. But she slowly straightened, although she didn't move the shotgun: it still covered Madigan.

'What d'you want?'

'I've come a long way to find you – Amy Ronan,' he said, noticing the involuntary tensing of her shoulders.

She stared at him, breathing hard, moved her left foot as if easing a little stiffness or pain in the leg.

Then behind Madigan the kitchen door crashed open and there was gunfire. He dropped to one knee as he spun, gun coming up – but froze when he saw Sheriff Blade standing there, smoking Colt in hand.

The man Madigan had gunwhipped and kicked to the floor was sprawled against the wall, three bleeding holes in his chest.

'Looks like I arrived just in time,' Blade said with a satisfied smile.

6
Persuasion

Blade said he knew the dead men as hardcases who hung around town from time to time. Usually if he saw them he hurried them along. He thought their names were Lobo and Ty.

The girl said she didn't know them at all.

'They must've been hiding in the house but for some reason let me start cooking before they made an appearance.' She flicked her gaze to Madigan. 'I have to thank you, Marshal. And you, Sheriff.'

To Madigan, this last seemed to be added reluctantly but Blade didn't appear to notice, preened himself a little, still trying to impress the young woman.

'You almost had me fooled,' Madigan said to her. The table had been righted now, the dead men dragged out into the yard temporarily, and she had made coffee. Madigan sipped from his cup, watching her over the rim. 'Standing up and walking to that filing-cabinet without sign of a limp threw me way off.'

She gave him a sober glance and he could see behind the plain look she had affected. The severe hair-style, no lip-rouge or colour added to the cheeks or outlines to the eyes, like some of the younger women affected these days, together with the baggy, drab clothing – it all added up to making her appear older and *homely*. But the beauty was there if a man looked past the deadpan mask – and the years fell away. Now he saw that she couldn't be more than the eighteen she was supposed to be.

'I can take a few steps without my leg bothering me,' she said quietly, flicking her eyes towards Blade. 'I have a brace on it and without it I have to use a walking-stick. I do that at home here just for comfort. The brace is annoying at times.'

'You are Amy Ronan, then?'

She nodded. 'Why are you here?'

'We think Mathias Griffin has escaped from prison,' said Blade. 'We don't want to frighten you, but it's possible he may try to harm you.'

She was as white as bride's gown, her hands clenched now. 'But – I understood he had died years ago! A bear . . .'

Madigan was glaring at Blade, swung his gaze to the girl. 'Seems it was another of his tricks to throw the law off his track. We don't know that he knows anything about you these days, but just as a precaution, I'm here to offer you any protection you may need.'

She was breathing hard now and some of the toughness had gone from her face and eyes, softening the features, making her look beautiful – and vulnerable. Madigan swung to Blade.

71

'Why would those hardcases attack Amy, Blade? That their usual style?'

Blade pursed his lips but looked at the girl rather than the marshal.

'Oh, they've been known to attempt – er – rape before this. But usually they stay with rolling drunks, or break into houses while folk are at work.'

'You never saw them hanging around your house? Or the depot?' Madigan asked the girl, and she shook her head.

'No. I might've seen them around town, I'm not sure. But I've never spoken to them and they haven't shown any interest in me that I'm aware of. Until tonight, I mean.'

'Almost as if they were doing a job.'

Blade tensed at Madigan's words. 'You mean – someone hired them to – molest Miss Kirk – er – Roman, is it?'

'Ronan,' Madigan corrected him. 'Yeah, that's what I mean. Maybe not *molest* so much as abduct her.'

'Oh, Lord!' the girl gasped.

'Sorry, Amy, I'm not trying to scare you. But I have to look at the possibility that Griffin could've sent them.'

She was shaking now and trying mighty hard not to let it show. 'I – I still have nightmares about that time,' she whispered.

'Don't doubt it.' Madigan's sympathy was clear even though his voice was so rough. 'It's the kind of thing that stays around for a long time.'

'For life!' she said emphatically, her eyes wide.

'Sometimes I think I'll go – mad, remembering.'

Madigan glanced at Blade. 'Better get those dead men out of the yard, Sheriff. I'll stay with Amy.'

Blade didn't aim to be left out altogether.

'I can relieve you later,' he said eagerly.

'No!' The girl spoke sharply, still fighting to keep her fear from showing too much. 'It's – I'll be all right. Really.'

'Sure you will. Because I'll be here to guard you. Okay, Blade. Best get your chores done.'

The small sheriff glared coldly at Madigan, stood, reaching for his hat. He nodded tautly to the girl and went out. Madigan was surprised to hear her release a long breath.

'Thank goodness he's gone!'

'You don't like Blade?'

'He gives me –no, I don't like him much. No real reason except he's so – so self-assured. He seems to think that any woman – of any age – finds him – attractive.'

Madigan frowned. 'He's made a pass at you?'

'Not – as such. Just things he's said. Double meanings, smutty.' Her eyes travelled over the rugged, scarred features of the big man across the table from her. 'And he's a killer.'

'Well, he is a lawman, and sometimes you have to . . .'

She shook her head. 'No, I don't mean that. He just killed Lobo in cold blood. Ty was obviously dead, with your bullet through his face, but Lobo was just coming round, groggily, when Blade came in and immediately shot him three times. I saw it while I covered you with the shotgun. Your back was to the room.'

'Well, maybe it looked like Lobo was trying to get his gun . . .' Then Madigan remembered he had smashed the weapon from Lobo's hand and the gun was still on the floor near the stove when Lobo had fallen, several feet away.

'Did they say anything when they came into the kitchen?'

'They – startled me, which was why I screamed. One of them said something to the other just then but I didn't really catch the words. Wait! He said – he said, "First time we got permission to do this, Ty!" . . .'

'Like someone had hired 'em to grab you, and they didn't have to worry about the law afterwards,' the marshal mused aloud. 'Any reason why Blade might send them after you?'

'No, of course not. Unless . . .' Her face straightened, a hand going to her mouth. 'My Lord, there *was* something! Weeks ago, before that awful train robbery. . . .'

Sheriff Blade returned to his office after making arrangements with the local undertaker to bury Lobo and Ty at county expense. The small sheriff jumped when he opened the door and saw Madigan sitting behind the desk, a cocked sixgun in his hand.

'Come on in, Blade. We need to talk.'

Blade blustered as he closed the door behind him. 'Kindly vacate my chair! I do not take kindly to this sort of intrusion, Marshal!'

Madigan's gun waved vaguely to the visitor's chair. 'Have a seat – and shut up till I tell you to talk.'

'Now just a minute!'

Madigan stood, came round the desk and, towering over the other man, pushed him down roughly into the chair. He whipped his gun barrel across Blade's face and the man was so shocked that he fell to the floor. Madigan stomped on his well-kept hand when Blade tried to draw his gun. The marshal leaned down and took it, ramming it into his belt. He hauled the dazed sheriff up and slammed him down into the chair again. There was a welt across Blade's cheek and blood oozed from a corner of his mouth.

'Are you out of your head?' Blade slurred, dabbing at his mouth with a kerchief.

'You're gonna be in pretty bad shape by the time we find out for sure unless you tell me what I want to know.'

'Goddammit, I've co-operated with you right from the start! Man, I even saved your life no more than an hour ago when that hardcase Lobo was going to kill you!'

'Couldn't do much to me when he was lying five feet away from his sixgun, Blade.' Madigan leaned over the man. 'You hired him and Ty to grab the girl, didn't you?'

'You *are* crazy!'

'Were you going to hold her for Griffin?'

Blade froze, colour draining from his face. 'Good God, *no*! I mean – I don't know what you're talking about!'

'I showed you that wire from Marshal Parminter

which said it was more than possible Cadey and his bunch had had inside information about that payroll train they robbed. *You* gave them that information.'

Blade scoffed, dabbing at the cut inside his mouth. 'By God, don't think Parminter won't hear about this, Madigan! I've never been so insul—'

Madigan's knuckles slammed Blade's head around on his neck, then the calloused palm came swinging back and spun his head the other way. The chair rocked and Madigan steadied it.

'You were given that information by Amy Ronan, as a matter of course. Seeing as you're the law here – and God help Albuquerque! – you were entitled to be notified of the schedule of the payroll train – and you passed it along to Cadey.'

'This is . . .' Blade winced and shut his mouth as Madigan's fist clenched and lifted menacingly.

'Maybe it was a regular thing, you dealing with Cadey and maybe other outlaws. But the point is, Amy knew you were the only one apart from herself and the railroad agent who knew the schedule, how much the safe contained and so on. I figure you were afraid I'd mention our suspicions of an insider to Amy, or Mary Kirk, as she called herself, so you hired those two hardcases to grab her and I reckon it likely would've been put down to Griffin – or those two killers from Cadey's gang still on the loose.'

He saw by Blade's face that he had come close enough to the truth to shake the man to his boots.

'You slimy son of a bitch! Putting on a big front of an efficient lawman, dotting all the i's and crossing all the t's – just a cover-up for yet another corrupt sheriff!'

Blade flinched as Madigan made as if to strike him again, but his eyes were blazing.

'You're so goddam smug, aren't you! Big, tall marshal, stalking about the West, gunning down the badmen, earning yourself a big reputation, bullying the local law . . . !'

He paused, almost inarticulate, his chest was heaving so wildly with his rage.

And suddenly Madigan felt sorry for him – not much, but a little. He spoke quietly, his own rage subsiding some.

'When did the Marshals' Service reject you?'

Blade curled a lip, his face twisted. 'Three times! *Three* times I tried and they threw me out. Told me I was doing a fine job as sheriff, that I was a good *little* lawman and I should stick to what I could handle!' He spat on the floor. 'The bastard who said that stood taller than you! Must've been almost six-six. Well, I showed them! I cleaned up every town I went to, town after town, my reputation growing. But they still didn't want me. I kept hoping and then – well, I'd had plenty of hints and straight-out offers from outlaws to sell them information I was privy to. After a while I thought, "Why not?" Being a good *little* lawman was getting me nowhere.'

'I'd heard about you long before I came here,' Madigan told him quietly. 'You had a damn good rep as a lawman. I was looking forward to meeting you. But you've turned out to be nothing more than a greedy snake, Blade. But you can live with that or not, I don't care. What I do care about is where I'll find Markham and Berry. I've a hunch Griffin is gonna want to contact them sooner or later. So, let's get down to it, eh?'

Madigan took a pair of work workgloves from his belt. He pulled them on as Blade's anger drained from his face.

When he arrived back at the girl's house she met him with the shotgun in her hand, double-cocked and loaded for bear. He smiled thinly.

'Good to see you being so cautious.'

She allowed him to enter, let down the gun-hammers but did not set the weapon aside. She was staring at him and he frowned, looked down at himself, saw the splashes of blood and the gloves pushed through his belt showing fresh rents in the leather, also red-tinged.

'Blade's a tough little rooster but I don't have time to ask politely.'

'Did you find out what you wanted?' Her voice was carefully neutral and still she held on to the shotgun as he pulled out a chair and sat at the kitchen table.

Madigan nodded in answer to her question.

'And what's happened to the sheriff? Is he still – alive?'

'Hell, yeah. We just had a short talk. He's banged up some but that comes with the badge. Except he don't have a badge any longer. I took it off him.'

Her look was sharp. 'D'you have the authority to do that?'

'Sure – I gave it to myself. The railroad agent told

78

me Blade had a good deputy whom he didn't use much. Maybe because he'd a big young feller, I dunno. Name of Chuck O'Dell.'

Her glance was sharp. 'I know Chuck. He'd like to be sheriff one day. But Blade doesn't like him.'

'He is sheriff at the moment. Blade's in his own cells. I've sent for another marshal.'

She was silent for a few moments, then sat down, easing her stiff leg and grimacing.

'Bother you much?'

'Sometimes. What're you going to do now?'

'Go see if Markham and Berry are where Blade says. It's part of my job to bring 'em in, but I've a hunch Griffin will try to join them.'

'Why?'

'Just a hunch, like I said. He'll need money and that means stealing it, far as he's concerned. He can pull a robbery easier if he's got some pards and Markham and Berry rode with him at one time. I've arranged with your boss to see you're given protection, just in case. So there'll be someone, armed, here all the time, escorting you to work and wherever you want to go.'

Her eyes flashed. 'It's not necessary! I can look after myself!'

'Don't doubt it, but Tanner and Chuck O'Dell will make sure you're safe.' He stood, yawning. 'I'm going to turn in and hit the trail early.'

She stood up, too, although he gestured for her to stay seated.

'I must thank you for – rescuing me earlier. And – arranging for me to be looked after. But I've been

self-sufficient for a long time now and I'll find it –
difficult to get used to someone else being with me.'

'With any luck it won't be for long. There're
hundreds of men in posses looking for Griffin. I'm
not the only one. He can't dodge us all.'

She said nothing, let him find his own way out.
Then he called, 'Lock up now. Your guard will be
along directly and he'll knock – two sharp, a pause,
two more sharp and then five quick taps.' She didn't
answer.

He went out into the night and Amy Ronan sat
down again at the table.

Madigan seemed thoughtful and efficient, but
there was one thing he had overlooked.

*Her own desire to exact her own kind of vengeance on
Mathias Griffin, the man who had robbed her of her entire
family and changed her life for ever.*

The law could have him. But only after *she* had
finished with him.

7
Wild Horses, Wild Men

There was a man named Huckabee who lived in the foothills of the Manzanita Mountains, not far from Albuquerque. He ran a small ranch there and made a better living than anyone would think possible, given the size and position of the spread. The creek was no more than a string of water-holes for most of the summer unless the rains came. The pastures were nothing to write home about and Huckabee employed no one, although the odd rider or two stopped by occasionally for a spell before moving on.

Huckabee owed Bronco Madigan.

The marshal had played down the man's part in a big rustling deal in Texas in exchange for information and that – together with a lot of luck – was why Huckabee was still walking free.

But when Madigan dismounted in the tumble-down ranch yard and Huckabee came to the door of his shack, he knew it was time to even the score.

Madigan didn't bother with more than a cursory greeting, sat down in the shade offered by the small awning along the front of the shack and pulled out tobacco and papers.

'Shell Markham and Zac Berry.'

Huckabee was a large man, walked with the gait of a grizzly, swinging his arms a lot. He sat down on an upturned nail-keg beside Madigan, lifted a stone jug from under a wet square of burlap, uncorked it and drank. He smacked his lips as he handed it to the marshal who shook his head.

'I need a smoke worse than a drink. But I wouldn't strike a match while you've got that jug uncorked, Huck.'

Huckabee grinned, showing uneven teeth. But he corked the jar. 'I dunno nothin' about them two. They was always too bloody for me, you know that.'

Madigan knew it. Huckabee wasn't all that tough and he wasn't a killer. A thief, sure, a liar, never a doubt about that, but a killer – no. Not that the man *wouldn't* kill if cornered, though.

'I've got a notion where they're hanging out. I want you to confirm it for me – and tell me what they're up to.'

'Just told you I got nothin' to do with 'em. And don't want to, neither.'

'You still help men on the dodge, Huck, and they bring you news. The big news right now is that a feller named Mayfield busted out of Flogging Creek.'

'Yeah! How about that, huh! First man ever to do it . . .' Huckabee shook his shaggy head. 'Sure would like to meet him.'

Madigan's steady gaze wiped the grin off Huckabee's dirty, weathered face.

'No you wouldn't. His real name is Griffin.'

That kept Huckabee silent for a time. 'You figure he'll look up Markham and Berry?'

'They used to ride with him. He'll need money.'

Huckabee nodded gently. 'So that's what they're up to.' He snapped his head up as Madigan made a move to get up, held out a hand. 'Hold up! It's just that – a man came through here couple days ago. We got talkin' and he happened to mention Markham and Berry were plannin' somethin' and they need some getaway mounts. I ain't got any right now but he said they're gonna go after a string bein' broke in up at the line camp of the Pueblo spread, near the Injun reservation. Tomorrow night.'

'And the Indians'll get the blame for rustling the horses.'

Huckabee shrugged. 'Give 'em a chance to get away.'

'This better be gospel, Huck.'

'It is. Hell, Bronco, I don't lie to you.'

'You'd lie to your own mother if you needed to, Huck. Okay. Let's go.'

Huckabee almost fell off the keg. 'I ain't goin' nowhere.'

'Don't bet on it, Huck. I need you to give me a reference and I need you to help me rustle those horses before Markham and Berry get there.'

Huckabee clapped a hand to his forehead. 'Judas! Knew you were trouble the moment I seen you ridin' in.'

'I'm not trouble, Huck. Not for you. Not if you do like you're told.'

Huckabee groaned as he stood up, shaking his head slowly. But he went into the shack to get his war bag and guns.

With some hard riding, and Huckabee's knowledge of the country, they made the hills behind the large Pueblo spread by sundown. There was enough light for them to scout these hills and locate the line camp where the mustangs that had been recently gathered were being broken in for ranch work. By round-up time, McClement, the big-boned, hard-headed Scot who owned the place would have a remuda ready for the trail and with luck his herd would be the first out of the county and into the holding-pens at Albuquerque – which meant the highest prices from the meathouse agents in Sante Fe.

McClement was no fool – and he did like to save a cent or two where he could. The set-up in the line camp called for four, preferably five, hands. But Big Mac, as he was known, had cut it down to three. When the bronc-buster had his leg crushed against the corral fence while rough-riding he had to be taken down to the main ranch house. McClement tore a strip off the man who had brought him in.

'Och, mon, I've *walked* through the Cairngorms with a stag's antlers through both cheeks of ma arse! I never needed a nursemaid! Yon laddie there had a *horse* under him! Och, he doesna even look very peely-wally! Now you get on back to yon line camp. Ye'll have to manage as best ye can wi' Morton.'

Seething, the cowhand, Hank Mulvane, rode on out and deliberately took his time returning to the line camp. *To hell with that miserable tightwad! He and Mort would just take their own damn time with the broncs now.*

So he dawdled and it was near sundown when he arrived on the ridge. He could smell bacon and beef cooking, saw smoke curling from the cabin's chimney. Had to be honest and say that old McClement did provide well enough for his men, saw they were warm in winter, had good grub, but for every dollar he spent on them he fully expected ten dollars' worth in return.

It was then that Hank saw the two men on top of the boulders, using field-glasses to watch the cabin in the dying light. *Hell, just what they needed! A couple of rannies on the dodge, looking for grub and remounts.*

He slid his rifle free of its scabbard and sent two shots crashing through the half-light. The bullets spat rock dust between Huckabee and Madigan and the latter rolled off the rock instantly, dropping down out of sight, working the lever on his own rifle. Huckabee was slower and Hank's third shot burned his upper arm. He floundered over the rock and by that time Morton was in the cabin doorway, greasy apron tied about his middle, working the lever of a carbine. He saw Huckabee and put two shots into the ground beside him. Huckabee fell sprawling, cursing.

'Judas! Take it easy! We only want some grub! Ain't et in two days!'

'You'll never eat again if you don't stand up and

claw a couple handfuls of sky, you son of a bitch!' called back Morton from the cabin. Huckabee awkwardly got to his feet, hands raised.

While this was going on, Madigan worked his way around the base of the boulder, spotted Hank, who was still sitting his horse, rifle at the ready, searching for some sign of his quarry. Madigan's bullet sent Hank's gun spinning. The man fell out of the saddle as he grabbed at his numbed hand and Madigan ran in, crouching, leapt over a fallen log and pressed the smoking gun-barrel against Hank's neck. He called over his shoulder to Morton.

'Drop your gun or I'll blow your pard's head off!'

'Yeah? Well, I couldn't miss *your* pard if I was Blind Pete from Pennsylvania!'

'Mebbe. But I'm willing to do it. Can you shoot a man in cold blood, cowboy?'

Morton knew he couldn't and tried to bluster but in a few seconds he dropped his carbine and Huckabee ran forward and picked it up.

'Okay, Bronco,' he called and when Madigan marched the dazed Hank across he said bitterly, 'Thanks for nearly gettin' me killed!'

Madigan ignored him, and they all went into the cabin. Hank and Morton reluctantly shared their supper with the newcomers, disarmed and uneasy, wondering how they were going to come out of this.

'You cook pretty good, Mort,' Madigan told the cowhand. 'Which one of you is the bronc-buster?'

'He hurt his leg, had to go back to the ranch,' Hank said in a surly voice. 'S'pose it'll be up to me now. Mort was busted up in a rodeo a while back and can't take the rough-ridin'. But I ain't no bronc-buster.'

'How about I do it?' offered Madigan.

The Pueblo men stared.

'They don't call me Bronco for nothing. Won't cost you a thing. Well, not much.'

'Knew there'd be a catch,' murmured Morton, a middle-aged cowboy with a lantern jaw and one wall eye.

'We ain't got no money,' Hank said. He was younger than his pard, bigger, too, looked tough but was a decent enough man, Madigan judged.

'Don't want money. Just want you to let us take about half the broncs you got in the corrals. And whatever I break in.'

'You're loco! McClement'll hunt you down! And he'll kill Mort and me!'

'Well, you take that chance. But I need those broncs by tomorrow night. Either way we'll take 'em. You want to try to stop us, you're gonna get hurt, I'll tell you that right now. You go along with us and we'll fix things so it looks like you put up a helluva fight and tried to stop us rustling your stock. That's the choice, fellers. What's it gonna be?'

They drove the horses into the hidden canyon that Hank had reluctantly told them about. There were about thirty animals in the herd. Madigan had decided to take the mustangs as well as the broken and partly broken ones.

Empty corrals would throw Markham and Berry off balance. The marshal and Huckabee had shot up the line shack, pouring twenty or thirty bullets into it, chewing hunks of wood out of the logs and shingles, smashing in the windows, making a pepperpot out of the rust-streaked chimney.

To McClement – or anyone else – it would look as if Hank and Morton had put up one hell of a fight but had finally been overrun by the attackers.

That ought to keep the cowhands more or less in the old Scot's good books.

When Madigan and Huckabee rode out they left Hank and Mort loosely tied up inside the line shack after overturning some furniture and breaking a couple of chairs to make it look even more as if they had gone down fighting.

'Wouldn't be surprised if there's a bonus in it for you fellers,' Madigan said by way of parting, but Hank had scowled as he lay there in his bonds.

'It'll damn well surprise me!'

They left a half-covered trail up to the hidden canyon, high in the Manzanitas. It would look as if they were in too much of a hurry to cover their tracks properly and Markham and Berry shouldn't have a lot of trouble following them, just enough so that it didn't look set up.

They threw up a temporary fence across the narrow mouth of the box canyon, using mostly dead-falls, but having to cut down two saplings to finish it off. The mustangs had followed with the main herd easily enough as Madigan had predicted, but they were restless now that they were confined again, even though there was grass and water coming from a small spring.

'They'll give away our position,' complained Huckabee as the mustangs shrilled and whinnied and kicked at other horses within reach out of sheer frustration. The partly broken-in ones settled down to grazing.

'That's what we want. But they'll settle down soon when they see the others are relaxed.'

'Yeah, well I ain't happy about them two comin' in here. They're likely to shoot us in our sleep.'

'Which is why we're gonna take it turn about to stand watch.'

'Judas, Bronco, I'm plumb tuckered! I haven't worked like I have today in a coon's age.'

'Do you good then. But I'll stand first guard. You turn in.'

Madigan picked up his rifle and a box of shells, went over to a rock and sat in its shadow cast by the low-burning fire. Huckabee dozed to the click-click of new brass cartridges being thrust into the loading-gate of the marshal's Winchester.

He awoke to the crash of gunfire, his heart hammering up into his throat.

Madigan was on his belly, still behind his chosen rock, but shooting into the night now, the rifle's muzzle-flame stabbing out like shrunken lightning flashes. From out of the night, from two different places – no, *Hell!* – *three* – *four* different places – guns answered and bullets ricocheted through the camp.

The horses were whinnying, snorting, a couple of the mustangs kicking at the fence rails.

'You'll kill the damn horses, you fools!' bellowed Madigan and just for a moment the gunfire paused.

Then a rough voice said, 'We'd rather kill you! If we have to risk a couple hosses, that's okay! Pour it in, boys!'

Madigan dropped flat, hissed at Huckabee who was prone behind a deadfall, between it and the fire which was no more than glowing ashes now.

'If that was Markham or Berry, call out, dammit!'

Huckabee, dry-mouthed, jerking nervously as bullets *whanged* off his deadfall, showering him with splinters, cleared his throat.

'Hey! That you, Shell?'

The gunfire ceased again and the silence dragged on.

'Shell Markham?' asked Huckabee, voice a-tremble.

'Who wants to know?'

There was relief in Huckabee's voice as he answered, 'Thought it was you, Shell! It's me – Huckabee! Why you tryin' to kill us?'

'Because you took our hosses, you son of a bitch!'

'No, we—'

'They're *our* hosses,' cut in Madigan. 'You want 'em, you're gonna have to fight for 'em.'

'Okay by me, mister!' called another voice but Markham snapped.

'Hold up! Strictly speakin' they're McClement's broncs, I guess. But we come a long ways to get 'em and what do we find? Shot-up line camp and two miserable cowpokes trussed for Thanksgivin'. They told us you stole them broncs. Now we want 'em. It's *you* has got the choice of dyin' or handin' 'em over.'

'Hand 'em over and *then* die, you mean,' scoffed

Madigan. 'I s'pose you killed them two cowpokes?'

'Hey! We had no argument with them, like we ain't got none with you fellers – except for the broncs. They wasn't yours in the first place, so what's the gripe?'

'We worked for 'em, that's the gripe! We ain't in the charity business.'

'Nor are we! Now what's it to be? There's four of us, two of you. We got you surrounded.'

Huckabee, white-faced, was staring through the night at Madigan's crouched form. He began to sweat as Madigan allowed the silence to drag. Just as Markham started to speak, the marshal said,

'Let's talk deal. Come on in. No guns. We'll lay ours on the ground.'

They argued for a few minutes but it ended up with Madigan and Huckabee walking over to the fire and stirring it up, the flames throwing light across their camp. Then the four outlaws came in. No rifles, but each man held a sixgun and Huckabee swore.

Shell Markham was a lean lazy-looking *hombre*, gangling, moved loosely, giving the impression of indolence, but his pale eyes were everywhere and Madigan had a notion the man could even tell him how much small change he had in his pockets. He was in his thirties and had a face that had seen it all – and was waiting to see more. Zac Berry was shorter, but well proportioned, moved lithely, like a cat on his feet, favoured a checked shirt and tight yellow neckerchief, though his trousers were worn and patched denim.

The other two outlaws, later named as Peak and

Smitty, were nondescript men of the wild trails, beard-shagged, wearing ragged ill-matched clothes and smelling of smoke and stale sweat and horses.

'Who the hell's this?' Markham asked of Huckabee, staring at Madigan.

'Name's Bronco, Shell. Good bronc-buster and knows hosses better'n his own mother's name, but mostly other folks' hosses. You know what I mean?'

'Bronco who?' growled Berry.

'Just Bronco.'

'Man's gotta have a second name.'

'Okay. How about Harris? That's as good as any, I guess. Long as you say I *have* to have one.'

Berry's eyes narrowed and his hand tightened on his gun. 'I got no use for smart-mouths!'

Madigan spread his hands innocently. 'You said I had to have a second name and I picked one.'

'Leave it, Zac!' snapped Markham as Berry's mouth curled into an ugly smile and he took a step forward. 'You boys dunno what you've gotten your-self into here.'

'We're waiting for you to tell us, but Razz-berry or whatever his name is starts wanting names.'

'Enough, dammit!' Markham was angry now and his pale eyes were flat and cold as they glared at Madigan who met and held his stare. Which only made the outlaw madder, but eventually he sighed and nodded.

'All right, let's talk over a cup of java.'

It was terrible coffee but it was hot and black and the men sipped it while Markham explained, mostly talking to Huckabee, but keeping an eye on Bronco.

He and Berry had been planning on hitting the Pueblo ranch line camp for weeks.

'Figured they'd have the broncs broken in by now and we need some for a job that's comin' up,' he added.

'You don't have to explain to 'em, Shell, for Chrissakes!' said Berry. 'Shoot 'em and we'll just take the goddamn broncs!'

Peak and Smitty nodded agreement: killing or not was all the same to them.

But Markham held up a hand, switching his gaze to Madigan again. 'Huck said you know hosses. How well?'

Madigan shrugged. 'Been bustin' 'em for years. Not so spry right now 'cause my left leg's just recoverin' from a bullet wound.' That got the outlaw's interest and then he pulled down his neckerchief and leaned forward so they could see the scar on his neck. 'Managed to slip my neck out of a noose, too, just before it tightened.'

Markham frowned. 'Gallows?'

'Lynch party.'

They were impressed. Madigan struck while the iron was hot.

'Those broncs. Only some are broke, a few half-broke, and a handful're still mustangs, though they'll follow the herd, but they'll make a heap of trouble on the trail.'

'Why take 'em then?'

'They're mighty good hosses, oughta bring top dollar across the line in Utah or even down in Mexico, but that's a long ways . . .'

'And you could handle 'em all that way?'

'Hell, yeah. Why not?'

Markham nodded, glanced at Berry. 'We can use him. And Huck's okay, good man with a gun as well as cattle and hosses. Long as they're other people's!'

'Never did trust him,' Berry said as if Huckabee wasn't sitting less than three feet away. Huck merely screwed up his face.

'Okay. Here's how it is. We've got a job on. We need mounts to get away, across the Manzanitas, and eventually up into Utah . . .'

'Goddammit, Shell, you oughtn't be tellin' 'em this!' Berry was really angry but a cold look from Markham's pale eyes settled him down again, muttering to himself.

'Huck knows these hills, right?' Markham went on and Huckabee nodded, trying not to let his nervousness show. 'He can get us across faster than we can find a way by ourselves.'

'And I know the back trails to Utah,' cut in Madigan, all eyes turning to him. 'Man, I've been using them for years. Utah's my best market for wide-looped broncs or cows.'

Markham spread his hands. 'Looks like it was a piece of luck meetin' up with you boys. Okay. You're in. But if you want a share of anythin', you'll have to pitch in and help with the job – and I mean, you'll be dodgin' lead.'

'Sounds like the story of my life,' Madigan said and Huckabee gave a sickly grin.

'Sure. Count us in.'

'For this job only,' Zac Berry said, his face insistent

as he looked at Markham. 'We're meetin' someone and he'll decide whether you stay or go. You don't like it, you can eat a couple bullets now and it's settled.'

Huckabee tensed. Madigan smiled thinly at Berry, glanced at Markham.

'Feisty son of a bitch, ain't he?'

'Listen, I've had a bellyful of you, mister!'

Berry snapped his gun up, hammer cocking – and then Madigan's sixgun blasted across the clearing. The outlaw twisted violently, his right arm jerking, the Colt falling from fingers that could no longer hold its weight.

'Judas priest!' breathed Smitty, backing up a pace or two. 'I never even seen him *move*!'

Peak ran a tongue around his lips and Markham watched Madigan warily as Berry fell to one knee, sobbing in pain, blood dripping from his fingers.

'You bust my gun-arm!' he gritted.

'Could've put that shot smack between your eyes. You oughta thank me, not cuss me. You're still alive, ain't you?'

Markham nodded gently, pale eyes still on the marshal. 'Looks like you're a good man to have around, Bronco.'

'Only if I'm on your side,' Madigan told him, and smiled coldly.

8
Dead Stop

Sheriff Blade was humiliated and he didn't aim to take it lying down. Then he snorted quietly at the thought for he was stretched out full length on a narrow bunk in one of his own cells in Albuquerque.

'Damn Madigan to *hell*!' he said aloud, sitting up, groaning softly as the motion disturbed the aches in his muscles and joints. Man, he hadn't taken a beating like that in a lo-oooong time. Mind, he'd handed out plenty, some worse, but Madigan was one of the coldest bastards Blade had ever encountered and he felt the involuntary wrench deep in his guts just at the memory.

But he didn't aim to just sit back and take it. Hell, if Griffin heard about it – *and* he would, he was uncanny that way – well, Blade reckoned the man would cut him to pieces before killing him. At least Madigan had left him alive and that damn marshal would live to regret *that*!

'Chuck!' he called, gripping the bars on the doors

of the cell. 'Chuck O'Dell, you two-timing sonuver! Come here!'

He didn't know what time it was and didn't care. If he had to rouse the deputy out of his bed that was just too bad. He shouted again, picked up his tin cup and rattled it across the bars until the sleepy-eyed young deputy came stumbling down the passage, holding his trousers up with one hand, his sixgun in the other. His torso was bare, gleaming with a thin film of sweat, and his bright yellow hair was standing out all over his head. He stifled a yawn.

'What you want, Sheriff?' O'Dell stopped a couple of feet from the bars, still trying to focus through the sleep he hadn't yet fully shaken off.

'The hell you think I want? I want outta here!'

Chuck shook his head. 'No can do. Marshal Madigan said to hold you here till another marshal comes for you.'

'Ah, hell, Chuck, you didn't believe him, did you, feller?' Blade forced a laugh, tried to punch the deputy lightly on the shoulder through the bars but O'Dell wasn't close enough. 'Hey, couldn't you see through him? He's *jealous* Chuck! Jealous of me and that cripple gal, Mary Kirk.'

O'Dell frowned, puzzled – but interested – now. 'How? I don't get that, Sheriff.'

He was still calling Blade 'sheriff' so maybe that was a good sign. Aloud, Blade said, 'Hell, there's nothing in it, you know that. I just been kind of looking out for her in my own way. She's a sad little creature, and, well, I guess she kind of got to me, you know?'

He knew damn well Chuck would savvy that

97

because the lanky deputy had been smitten with Mary Kirk since she had first arrived. But he was too clumsy and shy to do anything about it. Just preferred to worship her from afar.

'Look, Chuck, Madigan knew her under another name – her real name, Amy Ronan. That's why she came here and changed it to Mary Kirk, to get away from him.'

'What – what'd he do?'

Blade shrugged. 'Whatever it was, it scared that little girl half out of her wits. He told me when he was beating the hell outta me that if he couldn't have her no one would. That's why he made up them stories about me being in league with this Cadey and his old gang, Markham and Berry. It's his job to go after them and he wants me outta circulation while he does it. He'll come back and then Mary'll *have* to go with him whether she wants to or not.'

'She don't have to do nothin' she don't want to!' Chuck said, showing some fire, fully awake now. 'Hell, I'll see to that! He can't come ridin' roughshod over folk just 'cause he packs a marshal's star.'

Blade sighed, winced and rubbed his ribs. 'Well, he's doing a pretty good job of it so far. I think he's busted my ribs, Chuck. Reckon you could get the doc to come take a look? Something's grating there and I keep tasting blood in the back of my throat, I think I'm bleeding inside. He near kicked me to death. He's a real mean one.'

Chuck was wavering and Blade smiled inwardly.

*Just a little more work and he'd have the boy on his side. Just
– a – little – more. . . .*

Shell Markham was impressed with this Bronco. He
wouldn't let on, of course, but the man seemed to
know what he was about, no doubt of it.

He savvied horses and he knew trails and he was
good at picking campsites that gave maximum
protection from both weather and scouting posses.
He used plenty of tinder and only dried-out drift-
wood for the camp-fire, because it burned down to
clean white ash and didn't leave a fog of smoke to
mark its origin. He dug a small hole by each camp-
fire, lined it with leaves or bark and filled it with river
or creek water – handy if the fire had to be doused in
a hurry.

Markham had figured it was a little bit strange that
the horses, both mustangs and the broken-in ones,
seemed hardly to wet their muzzles at water stops. He
argued with Madigan over it, saying they had to make
sure the animals drank deeply before they moved on
to the next water.

'What if we have to pass it up for some reason?' he
pressed.

Madigan had shaken his head. 'No matter. These
broncs around here have a lot of Spanish *mesteño*
blood in 'em and they're a breed that naturally
rations their water. They know they travel better without extra gallons slopping around in their bellies
that they're just gonna have to piss away.'

Markham and Berry were sceptical, but Madigan

was proved right and they made good time going deep into the Manzanitas.

'We'll be clear of the hills tomorrow,' Madigan announced at the camp that night and wondered why Markham and Berry jerked their heads up so sharply.

'Whoa!' Markham said. Zac Berry had taken to remaining silent, dwelling on the pain in his wounded arm, glaring his hatred at Madigan but not putting it into words – not that he had to, not with those deadly eyes. 'We don't want to clear the hills *too* soon.'

Madigan frowned. 'Why didn't you say?'

'We're sayin' now,' Markham snapped. Huckabee shot a quick look at Madigan who wasn't fazed at all. 'We need to have these broncs strung out – or broken up, I guess I mean. We can push on the main bunch with the mustangs if they'll stick around, but I want two extra mounts per man along the way.'

'Why?'

'What we've got is a stagecoach,' Shell Markham said slowly. Berry tensed, but remained silent, watching his partner closely. 'Carryin' an army payroll for Fort Henderson up near Arroyo Hondo.'

'I know Henderson and it's a fair piece north. But why would the army ship a payroll on a civilian stage?'

Markham smiled thinly. 'To throw off the likes of us, hopin' we won't figure that they'd use Wells Fargo. They're runnin' a decoy, of course, armed patrol and all, along the regular El Rito trail, but they ain't carrying no payroll.'

'They'll have men on board that stage.'

'Hell, yeah! The shotgun guard is army, so are the passengers. But we can handle them. We hit 'em, grab the express box and clear away into the hills, where we'll have fresh mounts stashed and another lot waitin' north of Los Alamos. We'll travel a lot faster than any posse.'

Bronco Madigan was aware of Huckabee's discomfort; the man didn't care for organized hold-ups involving resistance. Lonely ranches and solitary travellers were more in his line.

'You do that, a blind man can see you'll be heading into the Continental Divide and they'll close it off. They've got plenty of men to do it.'

Shell Markham laughed, Peak and Smitty grinned, but Berry still continued to look sourly at Madigan.

'Sure. But we got *you* now to take us up the back trails into Utah, so let 'em search the Divide all they want.'

Madigan nodded slowly. 'Who goes and who stays?'

'Huck plants the hosses and waits with the main bunch. You come along with me and the boys.' The outlaw grinned. 'Just so you get your bloodin', you savvy?'

Madigan savvied: he either took an active part in the robbery or they would leave his corpse at the stagecoach.

'You gotta stop that stage first,' he pointed out quietly and this time Berry spoke.

'That's just what we aim to do, smart-mouth, and you got any sense, you'll watch close, an' you might

101

learn somethin'.' He twisted his mouth into a crooked grin. 'It'll be a change not havin' you tell *us* what to do for once!'

There was a stage, all right, but there was no payroll box, and no army personnel on board.

It didn't really surprise Madigan because, while he had known the army to use a civilian stageline before to carry its express boxes, this wasn't the way they went about it. Just loading the stage with soldiers disguised as passengers in itself would be enough to start folk gossiping, and talk about a special run would be the last thing the army wanted.

But just because it wasn't a payroll run, didn't mean that Markham's bunch could stop it anywhere they like without some sort of trouble.

And they were ready for it. Ready to kill.

And Madigan was powerless to stop them.

What caught him unawares was that Markham was talking to him behind some boulders, while Berry, Peak and Smitty went on towards the trail where the stage was expected. It was near the top of a steep rise in the Manzanitas, which seemed as good a place as any to waylay the Concord while the ream was labouring.

But the first Madigan even knew about the stage coming was when the guns fired in a ragged volley.

He snapped his head around to Markham who was smiling crookedly. 'That's your stage stopped dead in its tracks, Bronco. Ride along and see what other surprises we got for you.'

Madigan's mouth was tight and his belly felt knotted as they urged their mounts around the boulders. The rifles were still shooting and horses were screaming and shrilling. A man cursed and sixguns joined the racket. Then Madigan rounded the rocks, hard into the dust already raised by Shell Markham.

The marshal reined down, sliding his rifle free of the scabbard, levering in a shell. But he held his fire.

He was too late to do anything. Three of the coach team lay dead, while another horse thrashed and whinnied in agony. Only two horses, still in the traces, were alive but they were plunging and jerking, wrenching the Concord from side to side.

The driver hung over the brakebar, arms dangling, still, blood-patches on the back of his jacket. A man sprawled unmoving in the dust of the trail, a shotgun a few feet away: the guard. Another man's body hung half in, half out of the swinging door on one side, his limp hand trailing in the dust, a sixgun on the ground, brushed by his lifeless fingers.

The man was grey-haired and looked at least sixty.

'That's no army man!' snapped Madigan and Markham arched his eyebrows.

'Well, now, what would the army be doing sending their men by civilian stage, Bronco?' The man's tone was mocking and he could barely stifle a laugh. 'Aw, come on. Don't be like that! We din' know you from a dog's droppin'. You think we'd trust you blind to come with us on a payroll raid?'

Madigan was seething, had to fight down the urge to kill them all. 'Seems you stopped your stage, anyway – whatever's on board. If they're civilians, you better tell Berry and the others to quit killing them.'

103

Markham's face tightened. 'I'd *better*? Let me tell you, Bronco, you'd *better* watch that mouth of yours, or you could join the dead ones right now!'

Bronco swung the rifle and the barrel cracked across Markham's head, knocking him out of the saddle. Before he hit the ground, Madigan spurred forward, rammed his mount into Smitty's and sent man and horse flailing in the dust. He spun and sent Peak cartwheeling over his horse's rump with a wide swing of the rifle. Then he wrenched the reins and brought his horse around to face Berry. The man had his rifle up to his shoulder, one-handed, sighting swiftly before he triggered.

The lead burned air beside Madigan's face as he launched himself from the saddle. He carried Berry over and backwards and they struck the ground with enough force to smash the air out of their lungs. Berry landed on his wounded arm and screamed in pain, groggy, rolling aside. Madigan came up to his knees and as the man tried to kick him, dodged and smashed a fist into Berry's face. The outlaw went limp and Madigan thrust upright as Markham came running in, grabbing at his sixgun. Madigan's Colt came up and Markham, remembering how the man had nailed Berry, dropped his gun and clawed air.

'*Wait!*' he yelled.

Madigan only just kept from shooting him and as he strode forward, a gun blasted from the stage and a bullet kicked gravel between his boots. He twisted towards the stage, bending to one knee, but saw a man standing by the door, smoking Colt in hand, hammer cocked, pointing the gun at him.

'Uh-uh, mister!' the man said quietly. 'You're too good a man to have to shoot but you want it that way, I'll do it.'

Madigan froze, just long enough for Markham to kick the gun from his hand, then swing a punch to the side of his head, knocking him sprawling. Markham kicked him in the side twice and the other man standing by the stage said,

'Who the hell is he, Shell? He moved like a goddamn hurricane.'

'Calls himself Bronco!' Markham gasped, dabbing at a split lip. 'Bastard's good, all right.'

'He one of us?'

'Sort of. He's been rustlin' broncs with Huckabee. Knows his game, too. He can get us to Utah quick.'

The man nodded, put up the sixgun, dropped it into a holster. There was a moan behind him in the coach and he whirled, the gun blurring up and blasting twice.

'Thought I nailed that sonuver dead centre when the stage run up on to the team your downed,' the man said in an annoyed tone. He peered into the coach, lifted the gun and fired once more. '*That* oughta hold him.'

Madigan was on his feet properly, now, watching with narrowed eyes. This man who had just so casually killed one of his fellow travellers was about five-ten tall, a mite on the rawboned side but there was a hint of steel muscles in his movements. His beard-shagged face was pleasant enough but Madigan read death and utter ruthlessness in those eyes. He felt a kick in his belly, hoping his suspicions were wrong.

Then Markham, still holding the corner of a kerchief against his split lip, smiled crookedly and said,

'Bronco, I'd like to have you meet my old boss, Ma—'

Before Markham could say anything else the man stepped forward, smiling pleasantly as he thrust out his right hand towards Madigan.

'Never mind about me, Bronco. I just gotta say you impressed the hell outta me, though damned if I know what you were about.'

Madigan regarded him coldly and it took him a few long seconds before he raised his hand and gripped briefly with the other. All the time he kept his cold blue eyes on the man's face.

'Just trying to head off a slaughter,' he said flatly. 'I don't mind stealing a man's money, but I don't usually kill him unless it's necessary.'

'Sure, and I go along with that. But this time it *was* necessary.'

Madigan swept an arm about at the dead men and Smitty, who was at last putting the wounded horses of the stagecoach team out of their misery.

'All this for – what? Markham here gave me some eyewash about an army payroll guarded by soldiers trying to pass themselves off as passengers. This don't look that way to me.'

The bearded man was studying Madigan's face and his smile had all but disappeared now. He had a new wariness about him, some instinct warning him that here was a man not to trifle with.

'Shell was just takin' precautions – as he should.

He din' know you. Why would he trust you on a big job like an army payroll for your first chore?'

'I see that. But what I want to know is, what all this was for. I don't even see an express box around.'

'Oh, there's a small one up under the driver's seat but there's not much in it. You're lookin' at what it was all about.'

'You?'

'Sure. Me, Matt Mayfield.'

Otherwise known as Mathias Griffin, Madigan thought, feeling that kick in the belly again.

9
On the Loose

Madigan didn't have a chance to make any sort of reply to Mayfield. He heard the scream of a horse, snapped around, and stared dumbly as he watched Peak shoot a stone-tipped arrow into one of the surviving horses in the team from an Indian bow. The animal fell writhing and bleeding, and Peak shot two more arrows into it, and two into the other horse that had survived. Then, as Madigan continued to watch, head spinning, the man fired arrows into the already downed team and into the stagecoach body, as well as the dead driver and guard.

Mayfield chuckled, standing close to Madigan now. 'You get it?'

Madigan nodded slowly, looking coldly at the man. 'Sure. It was an Apache attack. Or that's the way you want it to look.'

Mayfield nodded absently as Peak moved around, shooting the last of his arrows into the sprawled passengers. 'Not quite finished – yet.' He raised his voice. 'Hey, Peak! C'mere.'

The outlaw sauntered across, tossing aside the Indian bow. He wiped the back of a bony hand across his nostrils. 'Did I do it right, chief?' He grinned, showing he had hardly a tooth that wasn't broken or chipped.

Mayfield smiled, clapped an arm about the man's shoulders. 'You'd make a good Injun, Peak. But, man, you sure can use a wash. Just noticed – we're about the same size. One of my shirts oughta fit you. Get my war bag outta the stage and we'll find you one.'

Peak grinned wider. 'Gee, thanks, boss.'

He turned towards the stage and Madigan actually jumped as Mayfield's sixgun swept up and blasted two bullets into Peak's back. The impact hurled the man against the coach and his hands clawed at the sun-hot timbers, his horny nails making marks in the cracked paint as he slumped to the ground.

Mayfield, still holding the gun, turned to Smitty whose face showed absolutely no expression.

'Put him inside and do the rest of it.'

As Smitty started to heave his recently dead partner into the stage with the other bodies, Mayfield smiled crookedly at Madigan.

'Need the right number of corpses of the right size for when it's found.'

'Something to do with you being on the dodge?' Madigan asked tightly.

The bleak eyes narrowed. 'Thought you knew the name when I said it. Yeah. Injun attack on the stage, everyone killed, then set on fire. Left enough tracks for 'em to trace me to that stage. They find the remains with the right number of skeletons, traces of Injun arrows . . .' He spread his hands. 'They won't be lookin' for me any more. And I get on with some real business.'

'Which is what?' Madigan found it hard not to shoot this son of a bitch where he stood but there would be little point when he would in turn be shot by the others.

Mayfield watched as the outlaws picked over the pockets of the dead, Berry even taking two scalps. His nostrils were pinched and breath whistled between his parted lips. Then he swivelled his gaze to Madigan.

'Bronco, you done well so far. Don't push it. You stick around you'll likely find out about my business.'

'It's pretty damn bloody so far.'

'Hey! If it bothers you, I can fix that right now.' The sixgun pressed against Madigan's midriff.

Their gazes locked. 'I didn't say it bothered me, just that no one warned me what to expect.'

'You can handle it then?'

'I've handled worse.'

Mayfield laughed, uncocked the Colt and slid it back into leather. 'Fine! Okay, boys. Get her burnin' and we'll head for the hills.'

With the fresh mounts waiting for them, they made good time into the Manzanitas and their camp that night was in a dry gulch far to the north. Madigan volunteered to cook simply because he wanted to get the stench of burning corpses out of his nostrils. He fired up plenty of onions with the pinto beans and sowbelly. Mayfield remarked that it was the best meal he'd had since before they put him in Flogging Creek.

Huckabee picked at his food, sickened by the way the others laughed and joked about the massacre at the stagecoach. He kept looking at Madigan who made his face sober and acted casual, taking it all in his stride. He felt Mayfield's eyes on him and knew the man was still assessing him.

'Shell said you boys're lining up a big job,' he commented, but only earned a bleak look from Mayfield. (He figured he had better keep on thinking of the man by that name – if he started calling him 'Griffin' to himself, he might slip up and say it out loud. For now they figured he didn't know Mayfield's true identity and he wanted to keep it that way. He hoped Huckabee would do the same.)

'Mebbe,' Mayfield said shortly.

'Well, are you or aren't you?' Madigan made himself sound impatient. 'I joined up to make some money. So far I've seen nothing, except a lot of blood.'

'I'm beginnin' to think that stage does bother you, Bronco,' Mayfield said.

'Yeah, I reckon so, too,' growled Berry, the bandage on his wounded arm now filthy with dirt and dried blood and spilled food. 'We don't need him . . . Matt.'

Madigan noticed the hesitation before Berry used the name. Mayfield didn't even look at the man.

'He's good with a gun and hosses and trailin' through the wilderness. What're you good at, Zac? Besides bitchin', I mean.'

111

Berry coloured and looked down at his platter, saying nothing.

'I did say he'd make some *dinero*, Matt,' put in Shell Markham. 'But I made it clear it was up to you whether he was cut in or not.'

'Yeah. As it should be. Bronco, you just set tight a spell longer. I got me somethin' coming up that's gonna make your eyes pop. You'll be glad you stuck around when it happens.'

'Long as it happens soon,' Madigan said levelly.

'Well, it'll happen when I say.' There was a challenge in Mayfield's voice and the way he looked.

Madigan nodded, deciding not to push it. 'Fair enough.'

He was surprised next morning when he was cooking breakfast to see Mayfield riding back into camp. He hadn't noticed the man had gone, for his bedroom looked as if someone was still sleeping in it. Mayfield saw the direction of his gaze and smiled as he stepped down, helped himself to a cup of coffee from the battered pot.

'Old habits. Some jails I been in you could do a lot of things at night, long as you left your bunk lookin' as if you were still sleepin' in it. Pretty good java, this.' He squinted at Madigan. 'You bother me some, Bronco.'

Madigan said nothing, stirred the mess of beans and the last of the sowbelly.

'You're one hard *hombre*, I can tell. I figure you'll kill between a man's heartbeats if you reckon he needs killin' and you won't miss a drag on your cigarette doin' it. The way you look at me, well, I can't recall *any*

112

man makin' me feel so uncomfortable. I don't like it, but . . . I don't want to get rid of you, either. I've seen you in action and I know I can use you. But I'm here to tell you, you got any notions of takin' over, cuttin' yourself in for a bigger share than I say, or doin' *anythin'* to kick my legs from under me, you're one dead man. And you won't die easy, I promise you that.'

Now Madigan raised his eyes to the man's face. It still seemed pleasant enough, but the eyes were burning way back like glowing coals.

'You've told me.'

Mayfield blinked, frowned. 'That all you got to say?'

'The hell else is there to say?'

'Thought you might tell me to go jump off a cliff.'

Madigan smiled crookedly. 'I'd *throw* you off if I thought it'd do any good.'

Mayfield laughed aloud and the sound woke up the others. Soon they were grumbling as they stumbled out of blankets and urinated and scratched and stared at Mayfield, wondering what had amused the man . . .

During breakfast, the outlaw made his announcement.

'I been scoutin' around. We cut across that ridge to the south-west and we're close to our old stampin' ground. Fact, I could see the tip of that tall rock pillar that rises near the entrance to the old canyon. We'll head there.'

Markham and Berry exchanged glances.

'Zac and me've been usin' that old hole in the wall. Fact, Slim and Potts are still there, waitin' for the La Mesa deal, Matt.'

'Forget La Mesa. We ain't gonna hit it. I've got somethin' else in mind, had it ever since I shared that cell with Cadey.'

'Hell, Matt,' said Berry. 'We been lookin' forward to that La Mesa deal, Shell an' me! We figured to make enough so's we could head on down to Mexico.'

His voice trailed off under the hard stare from the outlaw leader. He fidgeted, shrugged, muttered, 'Whatever you say,' and picked at the remainder of his food.

'You'll still make some *dinero*,' Mayfield said, 'and *I*'ll finish a job I figured I'd done ten years ago!'

No one knew what he meant, but Madigan felt kind of queasy as he had one thought that might fit.

The hole in the wall hideout was quite a way south and not far over the lower Manzanita Trail from Albuquerque.

When Madigan saw the place, he recognized a couple of landmarks that Blade had told him about when describing where Markham and Berry had been hiding out. Blade had said the canyon was called Candlestick Canyon because of the big, lone pillar of rock that stood near the entrance. Someone long ago must have thought it resembled a giant candle.

There were three cabins inside, one tumbledown and in need of repair, two in pretty good shape; a long low one and a smaller cave in the rockface, too, where corrals had been built and the two outlaws, Slim and Potts, drove the horses in here. Along the way, they had turned the mustangs loose, Mayfield deciding that they had enough mounts for their needs amongst the broken-in ones.

It had been a long, dreary ride.

Mayfield and Berry and Markham held low-voiced conferences frequently on the long trail up here but no one had told Madigan, Huckabee or Smitty what they had been discussing. The marshal was edgy: he wanted to find out for sure what this crazy son of a bitch Griffin had in mind.

He was afraid his hunch was right; if he was, he knew he was going to have to kill Griffin and the others. He couldn't rely on Huckabee for back-up: the man was a thief, not a fighter or a killer and he was short on guts when the chips were down. Whatever happened, he was going to be on his lonesome in this, and he couldn't help wondering if he could beat Mayfield to the draw. He hadn't seen any other gunfighter in all his years as a marshal who could get his gun out as fast as the outlaw – nor one who killed so casually and with such relish.

He decided that if it came to a showdown he would concentrate on nailing Mayfield first. In that split second when he was concentrating on the outlaw he would be vulnerable, at the mercy of the other five outlaws: Slim and Potts had the killer look; mean, callous men.

But it seemed to him that it was the only way. If it was his time to die – well, everyone had to die sometime. And he would take as many as he could with him.

'When're we gonna find out what this big deal is?'

Madigan asked at supper that night. Markham was doing the cooking and no one was in a good mood because the grub was lousy, burned or raw.

Mayfield chomped on a piece of tough mountain-sheep shot by Smitty.

'You don't listen good, Bronco. I said when I was good and ready I'd tell you.'

'Well, *I'm* ready – to listen.'

Mayfield pointed his knife at the marshal. 'You shut your mouth, mister! You don't crowd me or you'll find yourself crowdin' a hole in the ground!'

'That's as maybe, but I'm fed up with you and the others getting your heads together and not telling Huck or me anything. Hell, we're here to be part of whatever you're planning! We *want* to be in on it. I'm about broke and I need some cash. I can't sit around here picking my teeth while you make up your mind what you're gonna do.'

There was tension right through the camp and Huckabee's breath hissed in between clenched teeth. His hand shook and the fork clattered on the tin plate as he set it down.

'Christ, just take it easy, Bronco!' he whispered hoarsely.

Mayfield spat out the remainder of the lump of tough steak. He set his plate aside and climbed slowly to his feet. Madigan beat him upright by a whisker and they faced each other across the small camp-fire.

'You just dunno when to stop, do you, feller.'

'I'm not being unreasonable wanting to know what's going on,' Madigan said, his voice calm, unlike Mayfield's which was tight and menacing.

'I told you to wait and I'll explain everythin'. When I'm good and ready! But you just have to keep pushin', don't you?'

Madigan was ready to draw if it came to that but he sensed that while Mayfield *wanted* to kill him, he was still reluctant and stalling a little.

'I want to know something, I ask.'

Then, just as the outlaw opened his mouth to speak again and his hand twitched against his holster, a voice spoke out of the night beyond the reach of the camp-fire's glow.

'Judas, Griff, am I glad to see you! Was hoping you'd come back to the old hideout!'

They all spun towards the sound and then a man on a weary horse came into the light, dust-spattered and worn, leading another horse with a second rider slumped in the saddle.

The first rider was Sheriff Blade, still sporting some bruises and cuts on his face beneath the layer of trail dirt.

'I brought you a present, Griff,' he said, a little nervously.

He hipped in the saddle, smiling tightly, unsure of himself, and gestured to the second rider who moved slowly, head lifting.

It was Amy Ronan.

10
Almost to the Death

Blade hadn't yet noticed Madigan amongst the others. He was too busy watching Mayfield cross towards Amy where she sat her mount, hands tied to the saddle horn. Blade hadn't been gentle with her when he had grabbed her in Albuquerque.

She sported a black eye and there was a small cut at one corner of her mouth, a bruise on her jaw. And there was naked fear in her eyes as she watched Mayfield coming slowly towards her, savouring the moment, his mouth twisted into a crooked smile. Fear in his victims excited him.

'This is the kid all growed up, Griff,' Blade said, eager to establish good relations.

Griffin, standing beside the girl's horse now, grinned up at her. 'Well, she sure is ripe for the pickin's. Blade, I thank you. Know you brought her along as a sweetener because of somethin' you done that I won't like, but that makes no nevermind. I can

118

forgive you almost anythin', now I've seen this honey.' He slid a hand up her skirt and felt the twisted scar tissue of her game leg. She spat on him but it only stained his hatbrim. His grin widened and he twisted her leg savagely, though briefly. She cried out and almost fell from the saddle.

Then Huck could contain his rising panic no longer.

He jumped up and started to run, yelling, 'Bronco! Let's go!' knowing that it was only a matter of time before Blade recognized Madigan and gave him away.

His shout got the others' attention and Blade swore as he saw Madigan and whirled to face Griffin. 'What the hell're you doin', Griff! That son of a bitch is Bronco Madigan! He's a US marshal!'

Huckabee had stumbled in his lunge away, made a grab at Bronco's arm. He succeeded and as he staggered, he pulled Madigan off balance, just as the lawman slapped his hand against his gun-butt. He fumbled the draw but Mayfield didn't: his draw was smooth and half-brother to a bolt of lightning as the Colt came up blasting. The bullet slammed into Huckabee and smashed him down again. He fell hard against Madigan, knocking the marshal off his feet this time. Mayfield's second shot missed by a whisker but then he held his fire, covering the lawman as he sprawled, with the dying Huckabee pinning his legs, twitching and writhing.

Mayfield, his face grim and terrifying, strode across, the smoking gun-muzzle covering Madigan. His draw had been so fast that his men were only now clearing leather with their own sixguns.

119

Mayfield kicked Madigan's Colt out of reach, stomped on his hand, but the marshal managed to pull it away before the killer put any real weight on it. Mayfield rapped him hard on the temple, knocking his hat flying.

'Knew there was somethin' queer about you! So, you're a lousy goddamn lawman, Bronco, a *marshal* no less!' He kicked Madigan in the chest, knocking him flat from his half-risen position. 'I've heard about you. Bronco Madigan, the killer marshal . . . and they sent you after me, eh? S'pose I oughta be flattered.' He leaned forward. 'Well, you've found me, but it ain't gonna do you much good.'

'Nor you,' said Madigan. Griffin laughed and kicked him in the side.

'They say it's suicide to kill one of you sons of bitches, but, hell, *I don't care!* Oh, yeah, you're gonna die, Bronco, but you ain't gonna die easy!'

He swung a kick at Madigan's head but the lawman dodged, groggy, acting by instinct. He snatched at the boot and heaved. Mayfield twisted violently and went down on one knee. It was all Madigan asked for. A trickle of blood crawling towards his right eye from under his hairline, he kicked the Colt out of the killer's hand and brought up a knee into the man's face. Mayfield flailed backwards and Markham moved in, sixgun lifting above his head, the butt ready to crash down on Bronco's skull.

'Hold it!' Griffin yelled, spitting blood, more pouring from his nostrils. *He couldn't allow this to happen in front of his men!* Madigan, still in a crouched position,

120

ready to dodge Markham, flicked his eyes to the killer.

'You want to try your luck?' he challenged.

'I don't need luck . . .'

'I'm not a helpless woman – or a hysterical eight-year-old, you perverted bastard!' growled Madigan, making a 'come on' sign with his left hand. 'Let's see how you stand up to some real resistance!'

Mayfield – Griffin, now it was out in the open – smiled bleakly. 'You're a dead man, Madigan, whatever happens.'

'Then I've got nothing to lose.' But he had: no matter what happened, Amy Ronan was at the mercy of Mathias Griffin. So the only way he could make things maybe just a *little* easier for her, was to kill Griffin. With his bare hands. And as quickly as possible.

Griffin flicked his gaze past Madigan's left shoulder and nodded very slightly, so slightly that the lawman wasn't even sure he *had* nodded, but he started to turn. Too late! Markham hit him in the kidneys and as his legs buckled, Berry ran in and kicked him between the shoulders.

Softening me up, Madigan thought as he sprawled. Then Griffin waved back his men, stepped in with boots swinging. The marshal took the first blow on his upper arm, felt his fingers go numb and hot pain swirl up into his neck. He rolled and the next kick skidded across his face, tearing his cheek. He kept rolling, spun on to his back and lifted both legs as the snarling Griffin ran in.

The boots took Griffin in the belly and the man

made a loud *Ooooffff!* as the breath burst out out of him. He pulled up short, stumbling, and Madigan swung his legs back, with brutal momentum, taking the outlaw across the side of the head. Griffin skidded to his knees and, as Madigan sprang to his feet, Berry ran in, striking out with his sixgun. Bronco dodged under his arm and butted him in the midriff, brought his head up sharply and took Berry under the jaw. The man fell on his wounded arm. He howled and writhed, out of it for now.

But he'd be back. Griffin was going to get plenty of help. Markham came boring in but skidded to a halt as Madigan spun towards him. The lawman didn't stop. He kept coming, looping a blow at Markham's jaw. The man dodged to his left, and walked smack into a fist in the mouth. His head snapped back, teeth broke and his lips mashed. He clapped a hand against his ruined face, staggered to one side. Madigan lunged after him, kicked him savagely, and Markham fell, barely conscious.

Then Griffin came to life and took Bronco down in a flying tackle. They went over together, knees and elbows and fists striking. Madigan jarred with blows he hardly felt, twisted his head aside from pronged fingers aimed at his eyes, jerked upright and smashed an elbow into Griffin's face. The man's nose crumpled and spurted blood and Madigan brought up his knee again and sent Griffin flailing back. The others, watching, seemed uncertain about interfering now. They were wary of Madigan who was like a raging madman, shirt torn and hanging from his waist in tatters, spattered with blood, much of it the

122

other men's who had tried to help Griffin.

Bronco paid them no attention: he was concentrating on Griffin. *The man had to die!* He closed now, big fists blurring, hammering, smashing against Griffin's jaw, flattening his ear, thudding into his neck, ramming his heart up into his throat – or so it felt to Griffin – making his ribs creak with the impact of the blows.

Griffin floundered and went down time and again, working his way backwards on buttocks and hands as Madigan advanced like a grizzly intent on its quarry, ready to rip and tear and maul. For the first time in years, Griffin was afraid. He was hurt, suffering, knowing there was a lot more to come and that Madigan was unstoppable. Each time he opened his shattered, bloody mouth to shout to his men, Madigan closed it with a brutal blow that knocked the man down again.

He stalked the killer, stomping mercilessly, lashing out, kicking the man across the canyon like a crumpled bedroll. Then, as Griffin groaned and rolled on to hands and knees, Madigan kicked him squarely in the groin, twice.

'How frisky you feel now!' gritted Madigan, swaying, watching Griffin writhe and gag, face congested, his body twisted and convulsing with the worst pain he'd ever felt.

Madigan reached down swiftly and pulled him half upright by the hair, Griffin choking on a scream. Then Bronco clamped his hands around the man's throat. Griffin clawed and tore at those big gnarled hands as he felt his throat being crushed under their pressure. He felt the hot blood surging and flooding his eyes, forcing them to bulge in their sockets. His arms waved and flailed weakly, without co-ordination, as he made terrible gargling sounds. . . .

Then something exploded in Madigan's head and the world turned red. There was another explosion in his brain and this time the world flared with searing yellow before blackness crashed down like the night sky itself falling on top of him.

Mathias Griffin was a mess.

He was savagely angry even through all his pain and aches, mostly at the fact that he had been humiliated by Madigan before all his men. Griffin had always figured he could take any man walking this earth in a bare-knuckle brawl. But, by God, he had never come up against anyone like Bronco Madigan.

The man was a killer, there was no doubt about that, and if it took one to recognize one, then Griffin was eminently qualified for that particular chore!

Hell, all he really wanted to do was get up and go and carve Madigan into little pieces. It was an all-consuming desire, even stronger than wanting to take Amy Ronan at his leisure – and pleasure.

Well, he thought grimly, likely he had Madigan to thank for that, too. He had never felt so sick and sore in his nether regions. *Never!*

He had rallied as the men carried him back towards the cabin last night, the sour smell of vomit on his shirtfront.

'No one touches – Madigan!' he had gasped, eyes burning through the pain that flooded him. '*No one!* This time he's all mine!' Then just as they eased him into his bunk and after he had cussed them out for jarring his body, he gasped, 'The – gal! Leave her be! Anyone – touches her – before I'm – better, I'll gut him from neck to – crotch! You – savvy?'

Markham and Berry and the others looked somewhat disappointed but they all nodded and Griffin knew they would obey him. They would be too scared not to. . . .

They had locked her in the small cabin with the angled shingle roof. There were exposed beams in there with ropes and chains and leather straps.

And dark stains on the wooden posts and the earthen floor from past occupants.

Amy was still feeling stiff and sore from the brutal handling Blade had given her when he had burst into her house in Albuquerque, surprising her with the way he had overpowered the railroad man left to guard her. He had told her on the ride up here that he had 'taken care' of 'that idiot O'Dell, too', when he had finally talked the young deputy into getting a doctor to look at Blade's ribs. The doctor, too, would be nursing a sore head but he would survive – just as Chuck O'Dell would. Or so Blade claimed.

She hoped so, although she didn't know whether to believe Blade or not when he told her Chuck had only been knocked out and then locked in a cell with the doctor.

But Amy was alone now in this vile-smelling shack, hearing the rustling of rats and other night vermin, pulling her legs up and tucking the ends of her long riding-skirt under her feet. She clutched her walking-stick tightly. Blade had allowed her to bring the stick, too impatient to wait while she buckled the metal brace to her game leg.

She stroked the smooth wood in the dark, lashed out blindly once or twice at sounds that seemed to be approaching across the floor. But she didn't hit anything although the noise and motion seemed to make the unseen visitors freeze for a time. Then, once again, the scratchings and shufflings began and she pressed back into her corner.

To take her mind off any creepy-crawlies that might be scuttling about the shack, she thought about Madigan.

The man had almost succeeded in killing Griffin. He would have if Markham hadn't slugged him unconscious with that piece of firewood. But, in a way, she was glad Griffin was still alive. At least he would be suffering plenty after what Madigan had done to him.

Besides, she wanted to kill him herself.

She had never forgotten that terrible day when he and his men had arrived at the Ronan house near Quanah, and wrought their horror. Her own terror had been such that her small heart had almost stopped and there had been many times since when she wished it had; the sight and sounds of the abominable things done to her mother and aunts that day had been too terrible to live with at times.

But she had somehow come through and because of the kindness of others had returned to a more or less normal life, although her leg would always serve as a grim reminder of that ghastly time. Through conscious will, she had pushed it to the back of her mind over the years, and only occasionally did she relieve the horrors in sweaty nightmares, believing all that time that Griffin had died the kind of death she had wished upon him: torn apart and eaten alive by a grizzly bear. She knew her mind must be twisted to feel that way about any human being, but she had long since ceased to regard Griffin as a member of the human race.

And now – *now* the nightmare had returned and she was a part of it again – living it! – and it would grow worse when Griffin recovered from Madigan's terrible beating.

And what of Madigan? she thought suddenly, her heart hammering. What had they done with him? What *would* they do to him. . . ?

She hurriedly said a silent prayer for the salvation of Madigan and herself, adding aloud:

'And, Lord, if it is Your will that I do not survive this coming ordeal, I ask only that You give me a chance, however slim, to kill Mathias Griffin. Then I will gladly die in whichever way You wish.'

Madigan was half frozen and near drowned.

The stars burned with their usual cold blue fire high above and his head was filled with a roaring as unseen forces pulled and wrenched at his throbbing, aching body.

His head pounded and he knew there was a big gash in his scalp: it stung as the water surged into it.

Water! Hell almighty, he was lying in water! Almost totally immersed.

Water tore at him and wrenched at his joints

painfully, his legs in particular. They seemed as if they would be torn out of their hip sockets and something dragged heavily at his ankles. He tried to move his arms and then he discovered that they were tied to wooden stakes hammered deeply into the ground. He coughed and spluttered and choked as freezing water filled his mouth and nostrils, blinded him as it poured across his face.

Spluttering, gasping, he turned his head on his aching neck, pain burning across his shoulders. He looked along his outstretched left arm, past the slick, gleaming flesh to the ropes around his wrist, binding his hand to a thick wooden stake. Painfully, he turned his head and found that his right hand was similarly anchored.

And his body was almost submerged in raging water!

Slowly, his senses returned and his teeth chattered so hard he thought they would likely chip. He remembered the fight and cursed because he hadn't been able to kill Griffin. Someone had slugged him unconscious and his mind was a blank until up to a few minutes ago when he'd woken up in this water-race.

No, not a water-race. Leastways, not a man-made one like they build for logging. This was a natural flume. He knew where he was then: they had staked him out in the narrowest and most violent part of the creek that ran through Candlestick Canyon. Water came into the canyon down a small waterfall through the rocks high on the north wall. It filled a small pool, then overflowed through a narrow outlet, dropping steeply over a series of small ledges before forming the main stream below. These drops made for a series of roaring rapids, only a couple of feet wide, the water compressed into foaming, raging torrents by the narrow rock-studded banks eroded over many years by the creek that thundered down into the canyon proper.

It was underground water, surging up to make the waterfall, and it was freezing. Someone had had the notion of stripping him naked – he was aware of that now – and setting his body under one of those rapids, anchoring his arms to stakes driven into the earth of the banks either side. The weights pulling so painfully at his legs? They had to be rocks, tied to his ankles: he could feel the bite of the ropes now. They would be dangling over the next step down in the rapids, the flow of the water dragging at them and so keeping his body constantly stretched, every joint strained.

The Apaches were credited with having devised this water torture. He had seen one man, an army scout, taken from such a situation years ago. The man had had no rigidity at all, his limbs flopped like india-rubber: there wasn't a firm joint in the whole of his pulped body, flesh flayed to the bone in places. The army surgeon figured it had taken three or four days for the scout to die.

But he knew Griffin wouldn't wait that long. The man would be recovered enough by tomorrow most likely to show up and start his own brand of torture – and Madigan would be helpless to do anything about it.

Unless he could get out of this mess somehow.

He tried everything over the next hour but all it did was exhaust him and so he sank deeper into the water, his head sagged under the rapids and he all but drowned, coughing and retching and fighting for breath, twisting and writhing.

But by some fluke or superhuman effort, he managed to lift his legs despite the rocks roped to his ankles. The rock on his left leg, when he could hold it no more, caught up in a hollow and didn't fall all the way down again.

It meant that now his left leg bent and his body curled over to that side. It felt good, gave him some relief from the constant tearing and stretching of his spine. But it also did something else, though he wasn't aware of it for quite some time.

The water hitting his curved, naked body surged up onto the bank, swirled around the humps and hollows before washing back into the rapids. It brought dirt and gravel with it, scraping his flesh as it whirled past.

He strained against the stakes, trying to pull his body into a more comfortable position, hoping to move the rock on his right leg at the same time. Then his heart almost stopped.

The left-hand stake *moved* a fraction. He felt it give as he strained, just a little, but he knew immediately that the water swirling up on to the bank had started washing away the earth from around the wooden stake. *It was still doing it!* He felt the gravel and grit scraping down the full length of his body as it washed on to him after eddying through the hollows.

130

He twisted and wrenched, grunting with the effort, forcing his aching body into incredible contortions, trying to direct more and more spurting water up on to the left bank and around the stake. His numbed muscles cracked with the strain but he gritted his teeth and hung on. . . .

There was no real way of measuring time, but some of the stars had arced quite some distance across the night sky by the time the stake took an actual slant in his direction when he applied pressure. He kept it up, near exhaustion, flesh torn from his wrist by the ropes, and suddenly the stake angled enough for the ropes to slip over the top and *his left arm was free.*

After that it was easy. Well, maybe not *easy* – for it took a long time to work at the water-shrunk knots and drop those rock weights from his ankles.

But before sun-up, he was free.

11

'Madigan's Loose!'

There was a paleness in the east and its reflection picked out a few dim details in the canyon.

He could see the cabins down in the hollow as he sat there on the edge of the rapids, shivering, massaging numbed limbs, trying to think clearly but handicapped by his throbbing head. He had to get warm, that was a priority. It meant clothes or a fire and hot drinks, but clothes seemed like the best chance . . .

He had made the decision and was about to try his weight on his legs when he saw the light in the big cabin. No, not *in* the cabin, outside and moving slowly across the ground in the direction of the trail leading up to these rapids.

Madigan swore. *Someone coming to check on him!*

Bad timing. What the hell was he to do? He hated this need to think it out but his head was so full of pain and buzzing sounds that he was no longer capable of a snap decision. He plunged his head under the rumbling water of the top rapid, gasping at its chill, its force almost toppling him into the stream again. He put down a hand and it skidded off one of the stakes he had torn out of the ground. The sodden ropes lay beside it and its companion stake. Suddenly, he was thinking clearly. He threw a glance towards the lantern and saw it had progressed as far as the bottom of the trail. *Just about enough time. . . .*

The visitor was Zac Berry and Madigan wondered why it didn't surprise him. But he knew the man would take the opportunity to inflict more pain on him while he had the hated marshal at his mercy.

Berry was breathing hard when he stopped near the right-hand side of the rapids, the storm-lantern swinging from its wire handle in his left hand. He set it down and, gently rubbing his wounded arm, walked to the edge and looked down at Madigan where he lay with the water surging over him, spread-eagled, hand roped to the stakes, legs lost in the foaming water of the next step down in the rapids, the weighted rocks dragging on his hip joints. Or so it appeared.

Berry grinned tightly. 'Good mornin' to you, Mr Marshal!' He bent at the waist leaning down to look into Bronco's face, mostly hidden by the gushing water. 'Hope you're feelin' well? No? Well, ain't that a shame? Would've brought you some hot coffee but it ain't brewed yet so guess you'll just have to go without, huh?'

Madigan said nothing, kept his eyes rolling upwards, making out he was only semi-conscious. Berry stood on one leg, ground a boot into the lawman's chest, twisting so the heel tore the flesh. A

133

little blood discoloured the water.

'How you like it, Bronco? You got me to thank for this. I spent some time with the Apaches and learned a few of their tricks. When they was wonderin' what to do with you till Griff feels more spry, I thought of this place. Perfect!' He leaned down closer and shook his head, still smiling. 'Well, you sure look poorly, I'm glad to say. But you're gonna be a lot worse before Griff starts on you! Long as you're still alive so's you can watch what he's got planned for the gal, is all he wants. S-oooooo, that kinda gives me pretty much of a free hand, don't it?'

He chuckled and edged into the water, soaking his boots and the lower legs of his trousers. He straddled Madigan and leaned down, the lantern-light glittering off the short blade of the open clasp-knife Berry now held in his good hand. He bared his teeth, lowering the point of the blade towards Madigan's left ear. . . .

Berry stopped, startled, as Madigan writhed between his spread legs. As the outlaw began to straighten, saying, 'What the hell. . . ?' Madigan tore the loosened left stake out of the ground, gripped it with the detached ropes dangling from his wrist and drove the sharpened point into Berry's side. The man made a sucking, gasping sound and his eyes flew wide as he fell to his left, legs kicking. Madigan rolled out of the water and wrenched the stake free. Blood gushed from the terrible wound and Berry lay there, dying swiftly.

Before the man was properly dead, Bronco Madigan had his clothing off, pulling on the trousers

134

with the wet legs and the boots. Both were tight. The shirt was torn and bloody but he shrugged into it, the sleeves too short, the shoulders stretching the seams across his back. But he didn't care: there was some warmth in the cloth. The hat fitted well enough but his main disappointment was discovering that Berry wasn't wearing his sixgun.

No time to worry about that now. He lifted the smoky glass of the lantern, was about to blow out the flame, but instead merely turned it way down. He left Berry's naked body lying on the rock. He retrieved the clasp-knife from the water where Berry had dropped it and started down the trail.

His legs wouldn't support him at first and he crawled, backed down the steep parts, holding his hat over the low-glowing lantern in case someone else was awake down at the cabins. But as the circulation took hold and his efforts warmed his blood his legs grew stronger and he slithered and stumbled his way down. He kept his eye on the big cabin and skirted it, making the small one where he figured they would keep the girl. He didn't know if she was guarded but when he saw the padlock and bar on the door he figured she would be in there alone.

'Amy?' he called hoarsely, wincing inwardly at how loud his voice sounded in the stillness of morning. The light was strengthening but it was not yet full daylight and wouldn't be for at least another hour, maybe longer. 'Amy? It's Bronco.'

Through the roaring of blood in his ears he thought he heard scratching sounds beyond the door. Then her voice.

135

'Marshal? Really. . . ?'

'Yeah, gospel. You alone?' *She'd better be or he was a goner . . . .*

She said she was and he told her he would have to find something to prise off the padlock. He remembered seeing tools lying around the corral cave, rusted and neglected. He found a pickaxe-head fixed to a splintered half of a hickory handle. It would have to do.

The long hours in the freezing water had sapped his strength, weakened his muscles. He had trouble forcing the point of the blade behind the lock's hasp, and ended digging out a shallow channel for it to go into with the clasp-knife. The blade snapped but he didn't waste breath on cussing. The pick's point slid in this time and he strained upwards on the splintered handle. Wood fibres cracked and twisted. The rusted metal wanted to slide up and over the hasp but just as it was about to jump free, it bit in and the bolts drew out of the wood with a cracking sound. The hasp swung away so suddenly that he fell against the door.

The girl opened it and he stumbled into the cabin. She had her walking-stick pointed menacingly, as if to spear him, but lowered it when she confirmed his identity.

'Can you ride?'

'Of course I can! It's not comfortable without my brace but I can ride all right.' She gestured to a dark corner. 'They threw your belongings over there. There's no gun but some spare clothes . . .'

'I'll get into them when we're out of here,' he said,

picking up his war bag, wishing there was a spare gun in it. 'C'mon.'

He grasped her hand and dragged her awkwardly towards the corral cave, making little allowance for her handicap. The poles slid free easily but the horses simply stood there, watching him. He quickly saddled two and helped her up.

He held the stirrup and guided the foot of her game leg into the ox-bow but he could see she resented his help. *Too bad.* He ran back and removed the locking-bar from the cabin door, then led her horse and his own across the ground. He pointed to the trail leading to the canyon exit.

'Go!'

'What about you?'

'I'll be along.'

He slapped his hat across her horse's rump. The animal grunted and started forward. Then he led his mount back to where he had left the lantern burning, turned the flame all the way up and removed the glass and the screw-cap from the oil reservoir. He mounted, rode across to the big cabin and tossed the lantern on to the low roof.

It thudded gently against the weathered, warped shingles. The oil spilled out of the reservoir and caught fire immediately. He jammed the bar across the door. It wouldn't hold for long but enough to cause a bit of panic and confusion.

Already he could hear someone inside, shouting sleepily, asking where the hell was all the smoke coming from . . .

By then Madigan was in the saddle and riding

137

away, still wishing he had a gun. He saw the girl going through the narrow entrance and minutes later he followed, sparing a brief glance back into the canyon. As he had hoped, the fire and smoke had panicked the horses and with the corral-bars down they ran out of the cave and scattered across the canyon, some already heading this way.

Before he was through the entrance there were gunshots back there but they would only add to the din and send the horses running every which way. . . .

The girl, her face white and anxious, was waiting for him in the timber beyond the canyon entrance, at the base of the tall rock candlestick, clasping her walking-stick across her thighs. She looked relieved when he rode out.

'Thank goodness you got away!'

Smoke was rolling up into the rapidly paling sky and he grinned tightly. 'Main cabin . . . let's get going.' They reined aside as half a dozen wild-eyed horses thundered out of the entrance and raced past. 'There're still a lot of broncs running around the canyon. Griffin and his men'll catch some sooner or later so the more distance we can put between them and us the better.'

They started down through the timber, the slope steeper than Madigan had realized. The girl had a little trouble in the saddle, seemed to slide from one side to the other a lot, but her savage look headed off his one and only attempt to steady her. She sure was independent!

He kept looking behind but there was still no sign of pursuit. *By God, with a little luck, it looked like they were going to make it*!

Ten minutes later, two riders appeared on the trail ahead, rifles in their hands, blocking their escape.

Griffin was still mighty sore and hobbled away from the now blazing cabin. His hair had been singed and the clothes on two of his men were smouldering.

The outlaws were coughing, naked guns in their hands, eyes watering, looking around bewilderedly.

'How the *hell* did Bronco get away!' demanded Shell Markham.

Griffin, massaging his throbbing groin, looked around quickly, doing a head-count. 'Where's Zac?'

Markham shrugged but Potts hawked and spat and said, 'Seen him take a lantern and go out before daylight. Dunno where, though.'

Griffin swore. 'There's your answer! Berry always did carry a grudge and I'll bet he went up to give more hell to Madigan! And somehow Madigan outsmarted him!'

'Griff!' called Smitty suddenly, pointing as a breeze blew some of the smoke away so they were able to see better.

They all saw the open door of the prison hut. Markham took a step away from Griffin as the man's face went dead white, absolutely bloodless, his eyes like burning coals. He bared his teeth and swore long and foully. Then he turned on the tensed, waiting men.

'Well, what the hell're you doin' standin' round here? Catch some of them goddamn hosses and get out there and *ride 'em down!*' As the men started to obey he added, 'But I want 'em both alive. Hurt, I don't care about, long as they're both breathin' when you bring 'em back!'

Down here amongst the closely packed timber of the slopes, it was still shadowed, not yet touched by early sunlight.

The two men sitting just within the line of timber had rifles up to their shoulders and Madigan reined down fast, still twenty yards away, throwing out his right arm towards the girl. But she didn't need his signal: she too had seen the riders and hauled rein, her mount skidding a little.

'Oh my God!' she said in a low voice. 'And I thought we were going to get away!'

Madigan nodded absently, straining to see the men.

'Who are they?' Amy asked. 'Griffin's men?'

'Have to be, I guess,' he said and then the closer rider heeled his mount out of the shadows into the trail proper, slowly lowering the rifle. Madigan felt his stomach flip.

'When I saw the smoke, I had a bet with myself it had to be you, Bren!'

Chief Marshal Miles Parminter.

12
The Star

They didn't waste any time: explanations could come later.

The man accompanying Parminter was Chuck O'Dell, and one look at his bruised and cut face told Madigan the young deputy had been gun-whipped good. Blade, of course. The girl kept looking at O'Dell as they rode down the trail through the trees, putting distance between themselves and Candlestick Canyon.

Madigan figured it wouldn't take the outlaws long to catch some of the horses and when they came they'd come a'smokin'.

He had no explanation for Parminter's unexpected appearance but there was time enough for that later. They were well in the clear for now and the tightness of Berry's sodden clothes was growing worse as they slowly dried. Madigan knew he would have to change soon. Then O'Dell spurred ahead and signalled them to follow him. He led the way into thick brush that tore at their legs and their mounts as it parted reluctantly and revealed the entrance to a draw with crumbling sides. They reined up.

'We can take a breather here,' O'Dell said. 'Not many know about this place.'

'Blade?' asked Madigan quickly and the deputy looked uncertain as he hesitated, then said.

'I – ain't sure. Sorry.'

Madigan was already dismounted and taking his war bag in behind a rock where he swiftly changed into his own dry clothes.

'Never expected to see you up here, Chief,' he said.

Parminter grunted as he dismounted, mopped sweat from his face. He smiled at the girl.

'Not used to outdoor work, Amy.'

She nodded absently, looking back the way they'd come although she couldn't see the trail from here.

'I'll keep watch,' O'Dell volunteered and Amy Ronan stirred, staring at his battered face.

'If you have any water to spare, that face would benefit from a cold compress,' she said in a low voice, glancing away.

'You don't have to bother, ma'am,' O'Dell said, flushing.

'No, I don't. But I – want to.'

Parminter and Madigan exchanged an arched-eyebrow look as the two young people moved into the thicket near the draw's entrance.

'You sent word for a marshal to come down and take care of Blade,' Parminter said. 'I decided to come for myself, seeing as you'd mentioned the girl was there, too.'

Madigan's gaze was steady. He waited for a little more explanation, but got none.

'Well, glad to see you. I need guns, Chief.'

Parminter handed him his rifle and a handful of cartridges which Madigan put in his shirt-pocket, buttoning the flap. The chief marshal took a sixgun rig from his saddle-bags and buckled it about his ample waist.

'O'Dell wasn't sure of the way to Griffin's hideout but the smoke from the fire you started gave us direction.' He glanced across to where Amy was working on Chuck's battered face. 'She seems to've taken a shine to O'Dell,' he opined. 'Blade really gave him a working-over. The town doctor didn't fare so well. Blade must've hit him too hard, cracked his skull like an eggshell.'

'He's sure gone off the rails, friend Blade.'

'He's corrupt! And he'll pay for his treachery!'

Madigan abruptly said, 'Who is she, Chief?'

Parminter looked blank, a careful rearranging of his face. 'Amy?'

'You know who I mean. She means something special to you, otherwise you wouldn't be here. Even that assassination attempt on the President couldn't drag you out from behind your desk, but this little gal did it without even trying.'

Parminter's look was almost hate-filled as he stared at Madigan. Then he straightened his face and said very quietly, 'She *could* be my daughter.'

Madigan blinked: of all the explanations he had

thought of, that was one that had escaped him.

'You're not married – haven't been in all the ten years I've known you.'

'I was married once. But I went away to the War. It was years before I managed to get back to my home town. Years – and my wife was pregnant when I found her.'

Madigan felt uneasy. He hadn't meant to open this can of worms. Now he didn't know how to stop it.

'She'd been living with some galvanized Yankee she'd met. The army had told her I'd been killed in the Battle of the Wilderness, she said. I was worn down, Bren, worn down by all the fighting and killing and having been a prisoner of the Rebs in Andersonville. Coming home to this was the last thing I needed. I just – rode away. It wasn't till a long time later I found out the man was named George Ronan and he'd been killed in a saloon brawl that was none of his doing before I arrived.' His face looked haunted as he added, 'I just never gave her a chance to say so.'

'Listen, Chief, I spoke out of turn. This isn't any of my business . . .'

Parminter held up a hand. 'I exaggerated when I said Amy could be my daughter. Of course she could-n't. She was George Ronan's, but I knew nothing about her until I was assigned to the case after Griffin had slaughtered Mary and her sisters and tried to kill Amy. Imagine my shock when going through the files I came across a tintype of Mary. She'd taken Ronan's name, of course. I'd had a bad conscience for years about the way I'd treated her without even trying to understand her side of things. And I thought all I could do then was see her murderer brought to justice and do what I could for Amy. But I found out she'd been taken in by good folk back East and they'd given her an education and far as I knew she was happy. I didn't want to intrude, so I took the easy way out and convinced myself she was better off without me. Then we got news that Griffin had been killed by a grizzly bear and I thought that was an end to it. Until Cadey got religion and set a new cat among the pigeons.'

Parminter's face was like granite. 'She doesn't have to know my interest in this, Bren. Long as I can see her right. It'll be some sort of atonement for walking out on her mother the way I did. Apparently Ronan wasn't a bad sort, just one of those hard-luck Johnnies. Of course, he left her without a dollar, but I didn't even know where to send any money. And then it was too late . . .'

'Marshal!' Chuck O'Dell called suddenly. 'Riders comin'!'

They crouched behind the thicket, guns ready, Amy pale and tense, lying along her horse's back, clutching her walking-stick, listening to the sounds of riders on the trail.

'They've got a damn good start!' someone yelled and Madigan thought it sounded like Shell Markham.

'Keep goin'!' snapped a voice with a good deal of authority. 'They get away and I'll kill you all!'

'Griffin?' asked Parminter, snapping his head around.

145

'Sounds like him.' But Madigan didn't seem too sure.

'Let's take them now!' Parminter started to straighten in his saddle and Madigan grabbed his arm.

'For Chrissakes, chief! There's six of them!'

Parminter frowned. 'Since when have the odds ever bothered you?'

'The odds don't bother me. The girl does. If they get us she's at their mercy.'

Parminter stopped struggling, swearing softly. 'Well, it's too late now. They've gone by.'

Madigan frowned. He had never seen Parminter rattled like this before, not thinking straight. The girl had sure put a burr under his saddle and she didn't even know it.

'They'll be back when they realize we're not ahead of them,' Madigan said, 'and they'll kill us an inch at a time if they catch us.' The girl's eyes widened but her lips compressed and he knew she was steeling herself for whatever had to come. He admired her guts.

'Then we've got time to set up an ambush,' Parminter said.

'Amy's still with us, Chief,' Madigan pointed out.

'Chuck can see her back to Albuquerque. I deputized that railroad man, Tanner. He's trustworthy and a good man. He's got men to back him up. They'll take care of her there.'

O'Dell's chest seemed to swell and his face was red as he said, 'I'd be proud to act as Miss Ronan's escort.'

Amy half smiled. 'I'm sure you'd be a fine body-guard, Chuck. But I want to stay.'

That one astonished them all.

'Out of the question!' said Parminter.

'You'd be best going back to Albuquerque, Amy,' Madigan told her. 'Tanner's a good man like the chief said.'

'I'll get you there safe, ma'am,' O'Dell assured her, still looking embarrassed.

Amy flicked her gaze around all three. 'I'm grateful for all you've done, gentlemen, but now that I am this close to Griffin I want to see him get his just deserts.'

'*See* him get his come-uppance – or *give* it to him?' asked Madigan shrewdly.

Her eyes narrowed and he knew he had hit the nail on the head.

'Should the chance offer itself . . .'

'Don't be ridiculous!' snapped Parminter. 'I won't have it! Now don't give me that kind of look, young lady. I will not even *consider* what you are asking.'

Amy bristled, eyes flashing. 'Who d'you think you are? You don't have any say in what I do or don't do. You may represent the law but you let Griffin escape ten years ago and now you're trying to make amends. But you're not going to keep me out of this! Damn it, Marshal, I survived that monster's perversions and now—'

'Aw, gee, sweetheart! Now you've hurt my feelin's!'

They swung around, startled, Madigan even bringing up his rifle, but way too late.

Blade and Potts and the grinning Mathias Griffin

stood on the rim of the draw, covering them with cocked guns.

Griffin laughed. 'You oughta see your faces! Talk about bein' caught with your pants down!'

The main cabin was still smouldering when they arrived back at Candlestick Canyon. It had collapsed in on itself and there were still flames flickering amongst the tumbled, blackened timbers.

Griffin, although still obviously suffering from his injuries, was in high spirits.

'All you folk to play with!' he had crowed on the trail back. 'Man, I'm gonna have me one real humdinger over the next few days! Hell, might even stretch it to a week!'

He had outwitted then simply by having Markham imitate his voice as he rode down past the entrance to the hidden draw, which Blade *had* known about and had suggested they check out before riding helter-skelter down the rest of the trail. They had several spare mounts with them so it had sounded like at least six riders galloping past as Madigan and his friends had crouched out of sight in the draw itself.

Then Blade had led Griffin and Potts into the draw on foot and they had gotten the jump on the fugitives.

On the trail back to the canyon, Griffin had ridden in close to Parminter and bared his teeth in a tight grin.

'Glad to meet up with you at last, Parminter! You gimme hell ten years back, keepin' me on the run all the time till I was able to fake my death with that bear. Always figured I'd make time to square with you some day. Now, just looky what's happened! You walk right into my arms!' He threw back his head and yelled at the sky. '*There is a God after all!*'

Then he had leaned towards the girl, thrown an arm about her neck and pulled her half out of the saddle, kissing her soundly on the mouth. She struggled and suddenly he thrust her back and yelled, blood running from his lower lip. But he smiled when he saw the redness of his probing fingers.

'That's just fine, sweetmeat! *Just fine!* I like it best when they fight – so you just get ready to fight me like hell!'

He didn't even bother to look at Chuck O'Dell, dismissing him as no danger at all, a nothing man, young and not worth bothering about. . . .

That was Griffin's first mistake.

Or maybe the *biggest* mistake Griffin made was not killing Madigan when he had the man under his gun in the hidden draw.

Griffin turned from surveying the smouldering heap of blackened timbers and ash and glared at Madigan who stood beside Parminter under guns held by Potts and Blade.

'You son of a bitch! I built that cabin with my own hands twelve years ago!'

'Too bad you didn't stay inside and watch it burn,' Madigan said.

Griffin narrowed his murderous eyes and snapped

at Smitty and Slim, 'Tie them two lawmen back to back.'

As the men moved in with ropes he glanced at Amy Ronan who was standing to one side, leaning on her walking-stick. He winked. 'Your turn's comin' up, sweetmeat. Don't git stage-fright now!'

He chuckled and Blade said, 'What we gonna do with this damn kid, Griff?' He motioned to Chuck O'Dell who was standing stiffly, obviously wanting to try to save the girl but not knowing how to go about it.

'Aw, just knock him out for now and we'll have some fun with him later. Use him for target practice or somethin'.'

O'Dell got ready to run but as he lunged away, Potts tripped him and Blade clubbed him on the back of the head with the butt of his carbine. Chuck grunted and slumped, stretched out unmoving in the dirt.

Parminter and Madigan were bound back to back by now, coils of rope around their chests, pinning their upper arms. Griffin walked all around them, elbow of one arm held in the cupped palm of his other hand, horny fingernails tapping against his broken teeth.

'Mmmmm. Dunno which one to start on first, but I'm still havin' plenty of reminders of what you done to me, Bronco.' As he spoke he stepped in close to Madigan and kneed him in the groin.

The marshal saw it coming and tried to turn to take the blow on the thigh. He was partially successful, but having to drag Parminter's weight around

150

too slowed him so that he grunted and grimaced and his legs buckled. Parminter did his best to hold him up.

Griffin curled a lip. 'Well, that wasn't much but there's more to come – and it'll be done better and hurt a helluva lot more when I get around to it. You okay, Parminter? Able to support good ol' Madigan that way? Ah, don't seem right for an old man like you to have to strain yourself . . .'

Griffin kicked Parminter's legs from under him and both marshals crashed to the ground. A couple of the outlaws whooped and Griffin's crooked smile widened. Then he turned his attention to the girl, walked across to stand before her. She was pale and strained-looking but her gaze didn't waver and he frowned, lips tightening in displeasure.

He slapped her hard across the face, turning her head violently with the blow. 'You won't be able to see me for tears right soon, sweetmeat! An' if you know any prayers, it's my advice that you start sayin' 'em. Not that they'll do you any good, but I got nothin' agin you prayin' if you want to.'

He gripped her fine jaw between cruel thumb and fingers, pinching up her face, making her full lips protrude. He pushed his mouth against hers and as she lifted the walking-stick to beat him with it, he swung an arm, knocked it aside, then wrenched it from her grip and tossed it from him. She stumbled and almost fell, fighting for balance on her game leg.

Suddenly Griffin grinned from ear to ear. He looked around at his men. 'Hey, fellers. You done

151

pretty good one way an' another. I figure it's time I showed my 'preciation. Smitty, you still got that old harmonica?'

Smitty, puzzled, tapped his shirt-pocket. 'Right here, Griff.'

'Okay. You been around enough saloons and dance-halls and whorehouses to know a few tunes. Give us "Turkey In The Straw" or "Buf'lo Gals" – somethin' lively. C'mon! *C'mon! Play,* damn you!'

Smitty fumbled out the harmonica after putting his sixgun in its holster and got the instrument up to his mouth. He wet his lips and began to play a lively polka tune.

Griffin nodded in approval, holding the girl by the arm now. He shook her. 'Time for you to earn your keep, Miss Amy Ronan. Give us a dance! *In time with the music!* If it ain't – well, I ain't gonna be pleased and I ain't too sure just what I might do about it. *Come on! Dance, you bitch*!'

Amy fell, skinning her palms on the gravel. She rolled on to her side and Griffin planted a boot against her buttocks. He snapped his leg straight. She cried out as her body was propelled a couple of yards across the ground.

'On your feet, damn you!' he roared, drawing his sixgun and shooting into the ground near her flailing legs.

'Leave her alone, Griffin!' roared Parminter, on his knees now with Madigan as they tried awkwardly to get on to their feet.

Griffin triggered again and gravel spat against Parminter's lower body. 'Shut – your – mouth!'

'He'll only take it out on Amy, Chief,' Madigan gritted as they tried once more to get to their feet.

Griffin hauled Amy up bodily and slammed her down roughly so that her game leg crumpled. But he held her and shook her, leaned down and shouted into her ear: '*Dance!*'

He thrust her away and Amy had no choice but to execute some wildly uncoordinated steps just to stay on her feet. The outlaws cheered and Smitty started up his polka again. As she paused, Griffin moved in and she hurriedly started a clumsy hop-skip-twirl kind of dance, tears streaming down her face. Griffin grabbed her arms and whirled her around and around in a wild polka, half carrying her. Panting he stopped, looked around.

'Who's next? Come on! Keep her movin'! I want her to dance, entertain us.' He winked ponderously as Blade hesitantly moved forward. 'I'll see she gets rewarded for her efforts later!'

They whistled and cat-called and jostled one another as they lined up to keep the weeping, staggering, gasping girl whirling from one to the other. They clapped their hands in time to Smitty's tunes, snatched her from under the arms of one of their comrades, passed her roughly from man to man, pawing her, tearing her bodice, beards scraping her face as they stole clumsy, brutal kisses.

Madigan was working at the ropes but wasn't getting very far. Parminter was swearing and struggling futilely.

No one noticed that Chuck O'Dell was recovering from his gun-whipping, blinking as he tried to focus.

153

And when he did he was looking straight at the outlaws roughing up Amy Ronan.

His first instinct was to roar in appalled horror but he choked off the cry and saw where some of the outlaws had laid down their rifles in their hurry to get to the girl. He began to crawl towards them a little at a time, forcing himself to move slowly so as not to draw attention to himself.

He had to pass close to the bound marshals; he fumbled deep in his trousers-pocket for his clasp-knife – Griffin hadn't even bothered to have him searched – and he sawed at the first rope. When it parted he left the knife while Madigan struggled to get free of the other coils.

'Wait up, Chuck!' Madigan said, knowing exactly what the inexperienced young deputy was going to do. 'Wait up!'

'Be too late!' Chuck hissed. Potts suddenly saw him and started to yell a warning about the din of shouting and clapping, the ribald laughter, and the tinny music.

Potts was the first to die.

Chuck shot him through the head and the crash of the shot brought sudden silence to the canyon. The gyrating figures froze. They all heard the crash of the rifle's lever as Chuck brought up the gun and fired again. Smitty staggered, dropping his harmonica, but he wasn't fatally hit. He clawed up his sixgun, shooting wildly.

But it was Griffin who shot Chuck. The Colt seemed to leap into his hand, it banged twice and O'Dell twisted away violently, the rifle falling as he crashed to the ground.

Then Madigan was free, kicked away from Parminter who was still tossing off coils of rope. He dived for O'Dell's abandoned rifle. Griffin fired at him and the other outlaws scattered, going for their weapons. Amy lay on her face on the ground, head half raised, dirt-smeared, panting, her eyes a little glazed.

Madigan shot Griffin but the bullet only winged the man and although it put him down on to one knee, he wasn't through yet. But Bronco had to swing the gun on to the others as bullets kicked into the dirt around him. He dived to one side, bodily, triggering the rifle one-handed, and Smitty staggered, going down for good this time. Madigan hit rolling, came up to one knee as lead showered him with gravel and braced the butt of the rifle into one hip, working trigger and lever. Slim jerked and danced, went down, thrashing wildly. Blade threw up his arms and staggered into Shell Markham who was trying to get a clear shot at Madigan with a shotgun. The gun exploded and buckshot tore up the ground between Parminter and Madigan. Bronco heard the hammer fall on an empty chamber and he tossed the rifle aside, threw himself towards Smitty whose Colt lay in the gravel a couple of feet beyond his lifeless fingers.

Griffin fired at Madigan and Parminter hurled a handful of gravel into the man's face. Griffin clawed at his eyes and twisted, firing at Parminter who flung himself aside.

Madigan got the sixgun in his hand as Markham

brought up the shotgun again. The marshal shot him in the stomach. Markham lost all interest in any more fighting.

Parminter, moving well for a man of his bulk and age, ran – crouching – towards the girl as Griffin hurriedly reloaded his Colt. Madigan swung his gun towards the outlaw and triggered.

There was only a metallic *click*, and he recalled that Smitty had fired off a few shots before he was hit. Griffin bared his teeth, snapping the loading-gate closed on the Colt and stood, pointing the gun at Madigan.

'Just one in the belly so you'll be alive long enough to keep me amused for a spell, Bronco!'

His trigger-finger knuckle whitened and Madigan threw himself to one side as there came a dull shot. Even as he rolled on the ground, amazed that he hadn't been hit, he had time to wonder why the Colt had sounded like that. . . .

Flat – like a hammer striking a plank.

But it hadn't been the Colt that fired. Amy Ronan was on her knees, steadied now by Parminter, her walking-stick in her hand. Smoke curled from the end of the cane. Madigan met her gaze.

'I've been carrying a gun-cane for – for years,' she said huskily. 'I've always been – afraid that . . .' She gestured to where Griffin lay sprawled. That was all she said but it was enough for them to understand the fear she had lived with all this time.

Parminter caught her as she sagged, his left arm dangling limply, blood running across the back of his hand.

156

Griffin lay on his side, face frozen in a contortion of agony, his spine shattered by Amy's bullet.

On the long ride back to Albuquerque Parminter told Amy about his marriage to her mother and how he had walked out on her and only years later began to understand what she must have gone through alone, believing he was dead, turning to the first man who came along and showed her some attention.

'I didn't know Ronan was dead when I was there and, later, I tried to find her but . . .'

'You didn't try hard enough then,' Amy said uncompromisingly. 'You could've found her if you'd really wanted to. You had the whole Marshals' Service to help!'

Parminter said nothing because he knew it was true. He had been devoted to the job of US marshal and he had allowed it to take over his life for many years. Hell, it was still the only life he knew. Maybe it was some kind of strange penance for what he had done all those years ago.

Then Madigan had found Amy in Albuquerque and he knew he had to go to her and help her. Perhaps it hadn't been enough. But that was something he would have to live with.

At least he knew Griffin was really dead this time, and Amy was headed for a better life with Chuck O'Dell when he recovered from his wounds. The kid wasn't the greatest catch but they seemed to love each other and Parminter had seen to it that Chuck was made official sheriff of Albuquerque. He'd even left some money as a wedding-gift, yet, somehow he felt inadequate, that he hadn't done enough. He turned to Madigan.

'Looks like "case closed".'

Bronco stared at the girl. 'I think so, Chief. What d'you say, Amy?'

She looked from one to the other. There was not a great deal of affection in that look.

'You've done the job you set out to do. I'm grateful and I thank you both.' Her gaze almost crackled as it rested on Parminter. 'But I can't help thinking that if you hadn't abandoned my mother, none of it would've happened. Now, if you'll excuse me, I promised to visit Chuck in the infirmary.' She didn't say 'goodbye'.

They watched her limp away, using the walking-stick, but it was unloaded now.

'I – think I might as well go back to Washington,' Parminter said quietly. 'Doesn't seem to be anything for me here. Though I suppose her thanks was – adequate.'

Madigan had never heard or seen sadness in Miles Parminter before. It confounded him momentarily.

'She's kinda confused right now, Chief. Later, she'll likely think about things more deeply.'

Bitterly, Parminter growled, 'And the stars might go out, one by one!'

'Well, Chief, someone told me not long ago that every man has a star to follow.' Madigan took his badge from his pocket and pinned it on to his shirt. 'This is my star. Amy's is in the shape of Chuck O'Dell, I suspect. What about you, Chief? Have you got a star?'

Parminter's face hardened. 'Stop talking bilge and let's get down to the siding or we'll miss our train. It's going to be a long journey so I suggest you start making out your report as soon as we get aboard. It'll save time and when we get back to head office you'll be able to start you next assignment right away. There's plenty of work waiting, I can tell you that! Come on now. Stretch your legs, that wound's not bothering you much now.'

Madigan smiled to himself as Parminter lengthened his stride and adjusted the sling on his wounded arm.

That was more like the Parminter he knew.

'Good to have you back, Chief,' he said quietly and Parminter snapped his head around.

'What'd you say?' he asked irritably.

Madigan merely shook his head and pointed to the train that had already pulled into the siding.

Side by side, they hurried towards it.